The Perverted Peasant

or

The Dangers of the City

Parts One & Two

Restif de la Bretonne

Translated by Richard Robinson

Sunny Lou Publishing Company
Portland, Oregon, USA
http://www.sunnyloupublishing.com

Corrected and Revised: 2024 October 29
Original Publication Date: 2024 July 16

ISBN: 978-1-955392-71-6

This translation from French is based on the *Le Paysan perverti, ou Les Dangers de la ville*, by N.E. Rétif de la Bretone, published in the Hague, 1776, and sold by Esprit, bookseller commissioned by His Most High Monseigneur, the Duke of Chartres, at the Palais-Royal, at the foot of the great staircase.

Contents

Publisher's Preface[1]

Addressed to the Bookseller

It seemed to me, Monsieur, that these Letters could be of some usefulness not only in the Countryside, where relatively well-off people read nowadays like the inhabitants of towns, but in the City as well. It is, in fact, very likely that well-to-do parents, either in the Capital or other metropolises of the Kingdom, are unaware in part of the risk that they run by not watching more closely over their children. This work could enlighten them.

They will find herein the story of a young man who, gifted with all the talents and advantages that intelligence and a handsome appearance can provide, lost his way because of those same advantages. This is not an isolated case; it is what happens every day. If some young men from the countryside succeed in our large cities today, it is because they are most likely deceitful, false, hypocritical, and limited in intelligence; they make their way sometimes, but at the expense of society's happiness, because these newcomers, deprived of everything, and imposing themselves on the world, must take from others what they feel they must possess, by various means that a philosophical eye can easily detect. Which explains the painful feeling that many men have on seeing these *par-*

---

[1] Publisher's Preface: the original publisher's preface.

venus. This feeling is not a blind jealousy; it is a real instinct, based in nature. Already some time ago a man of wit once told me that someone would write a very good book entitled JUSTIFIED PREJUDICES. I believe it: there is not a custom, not a law, nor even one of those general abuses that an entire Nation abandons itself to, that does not have a rational cause. Without repeating declamations against living in the city, I dare to advance that it would be appropriate, not to forbid inhabitants of the countryside from doing so, but rather to show them its disadvantages, compared to the advantages they abandon back home, and above all to convince them that a fortune made in the city is like winning the lottery; one hundred thousand people lose for every one who wins.

I hope, Monsieur, that this Work will enjoy some success: may Parish Lords be struck by the JUDGMENT that concludes it, and strive to realize it in their own lands! The State, public morals, and they themselves will gain thereby.

I salute you, Monsieur: hurry up with its publication, and exhort Messieurs the Journalists to announce it, more for the intention that I had in putting these Letters together than for its execution.

Summary in Eight Parts

Part One

Edmond, or the Peasant, arrives in the city, and he experiences displeasures there that do not stop. The corrupters begin to affect him, and his passions imitate theirs marvelously.

Part Two

The painter, Edmond's master, makes him marry a girl that he had seduced. The corrupters try to destroy in the young Peasant every notion of honesty, which they call the prejudices of the countryside. Edmond, already corrupted, seduces a young lady named Laurette. His wife dies of jealousy.

Part Three

The corrupters, and primarily M. Gaudet, indoctrinate Edmond, by abusing the truths of natural science. Edmond is in love with his master's wife, who is virtuous, and he dares to abuse the goodness of this Lady by declaring his passion for her. He has an adventure with a coquette, and gives to his younger brother a girl that he loved. He ravishes his master's wife.

Part Four

Edmond goes to Paris to assist his sister, whom a Marquis has ravished. He fights with the ravisher. He is so corrupted that he agrees to this Lord, whose wife he loves, keeping his sister.

Part Five

Edmond and his sister descend into the filthiest debauchery.

Part Six

Edmond wants to become a Comedian, an Author, etc. His sister changes. He marries an old woman for her money and is accused of having poisoned her. Strange catastrophe.

Part Seven

Edmond is condemned to forced labor; his parents die of grief. He gets out of prison and punishes himself for his desperate crimes. He kills his sister.

Part Eight

Death of Edmond. Means taken by his family to avoid similar misfortunes.

The Perverted Peasant

or

The Dangers of the City

A Recent Tale

Brought to light through the veritable letters
of the characters themselves.

Announcement Found at the Head of the Collection of Letters

If I have assembled this packet of so many Letters from different people, together with those of an unfortunate man who has cost me countless tears, it is with the intention of opening the eyes of my family and everyone who lives in the countryside to the dangers that youth incurs in the city. O my children! Stay put in your hamlets; do not seek to exit from your happy ignorance of the pleasures found in great cities; vice sets a trap for you, irreligion urges you to lose yourself; crime furnishes the resources, and misery, infamy, and the punishment of the wicked are often the result. Profit by reading these Letters, where you can follow the entire progression of corruption that takes hold of an innocent and upright heart. At first you will see the young Peasant prosper, but then lose, gradually, his good feelings; he becomes a libertine, a criminal, and from then on he descends into infamy, dragging his unfortunate sister into it with him; he loses her entirely; he rises up finally only to fall down even further. My children, a respectable father and mother have died for grief, and an entire family has been plunged into opprobrium... The miserable wretch recognized his mistake in the end and he punished himself,... but it was in desperation. I saw him, and it broke my heart; because this wretch, – he was my brother.

Signed PIERRE R***.

Part One

Our family is not distinguished by titles, nor by great possessions; we are peasants from father to son; but our ancestors were a little richer than we are. They founded the village of Villiers, commonly called Villiers-les-aulx, on a stretch of land that belonged to them. In ancient past, they allied themselves to the daughter of a branch of the noble house of Courtenai, who had settled in our cantons, where descendants in the female line, having become simple laborers, still possessed a freehold of that name, the freest in the realm. Our mother was born a *Bertro*, an extinct family now, but whose nobility, proven by titles until 1200, was to die out in the beginning years of the [Capetian] Monarchy.

Since the foundation of Villiers, our fathers were always laborers. They were tranquilly cultivating their lands when Protestantism was first introduced into France. They embraced it, and this was the ill-advised decision that sank their small fortune; for when the sect was outlawed, they saw themselves obliged to disperse throughout the province and even, for the most part, to leave the Kingdom. They sold their inheritance of Villiers for next to nothing, and since that time we have not owned an inch of terrain. Our great-grandfather returned to the Catholic faith at the time of the *Dragonnades*; our grandfather and our father were raised in it, and we, like them, profess it. Pierre R***, our grandfather (whose name I carry), had three children – our father and two daughters – by Anne Cœurderoi, a relative of the President of Parliament of B***, and of that same name; the two girls were raised by two aunts, one who was a refugee in England, the other in Prussia, who had come to visit our grandmother around the same time; and she, not wishing to hamper the faith of her children, consented to their being taken away. Our father, Edme R*** (may God protect him), married around this time a girl from a good family, as I have said, and whom his father himself had chosen, although her dowry was only a large fund of sweetness, virtue, and beauty. Barbe de Bertro, our dear and good mother, bore him fourteen children, and this benediction of God makes one think of that excellent father, who lived only for his family, who sought to give each one of his children a stable situation in the city, in compensation for the property he did not have and could not leave them in the country. His intentions were good (for he only had good intentions); but the perversity of the world caused them an unhappy success.

One day, as our relatives were speaking of their plans with a Bailiff of the city of V***, this latter person reminded them that our father formerly had been very close to M. C***, the Notary of V***, one of whose daughters had married M. Parangon, the Painter of Au***, and he asked which of their children they were planning to send out from the paternal home: our father had Edmond come forward, who was two years younger than me and who bore his Christian name, just as I bore that of our grandfather's; and when the Bailiff saw him, he said to our father what follows, while admiring the pleasing physiognomy of the child:

"Place him with M. C***'s son-in-law; I guarantee you that he will make his way: those hands are made to work with something more delicate than a pick or the shaft of a plough; and I would be surprised if he does not find himself one day in the city in a situation that surpasses your expectations. I will speak with Madame Parangon, who is presently visiting her papa, and who is as good as she is beautiful. Encourage him; it would be murder to leave a young man like that here with you."

And after having questioned Edmond, he was all the more confirmed in what he had said; for Edmond responded to his questions in a just and, above all, modest manner.

Eight days later, our good father and good mother went to V*** to pay a visit to M. C***, our father's old friend, bringing Edmond with them; for Madame Parangon, after the praises that the Bailiff had made to her about my brother, had asked them to come and speak with her husband. Edmond was presented, then, not to the Lady, for she was busy with her relatives, but to M. Parangon, who found the young man to his liking, and accepted him. M. C*** promised to recommend him as well, and warmly received our father and mother. When they departed, Madame Parangon and the other Ladies came out to see them off; but Edmond, embarrassed, blushed, and did not dare to cast his eyes on them. They praised his modesty, and when one of the Demoiselle's gave him a light pat with her hand on his cheek, he turned red like a beet, which made them all laugh; and Madame Parangon said to them:

"You laugh at his timid innocence, but one day perhaps you will weep over his bold insolence of a *petit-maître*."

She promised our parents to look after him; and while our mother was caressing Mademoiselle Fanchette, that Lady's younger sister, and giving her small gifts, she inquired about Edmond's character of our father. The good old man told her how that child was sensitive, obliging, although passionate and perhaps quick-tempered.

"He is sixteen years old," he continued, "but his passions are still calm; and may they remain so for a long time! His organs have an exquisite delicacy, as they say; it is for this reason that I believe he will succeed. He loves to read, and he knows the Holy Bible by heart; as for Latin, he understands it quite well, and even some Greek; M. the Curate says that all that is more than enough for a Painter."

Madame Parangon was very pleased with this explanation, which Edmond did not hear; for he was amusing himself watching the world outside the front door, and our good parents went away filled with joy for the success of their endeavor.

Immediately thereafter they purchased what Edmond would need, in order to equip him; and over the next six weeks our venerable father and tender mother gave him their wise advice; at the end of which time, M. Parangon having written to them, Edmond was made to depart on November 5, 1748: it is then that our correspondence begins; for he wrote to me on the very same day of his arrival in Au***.

I.

EDMOND TO PIERROT R***, HIS OLDER BROTHER

Having arrived at M. Parangon's house.

MY DEAR BROTHER,

I pick up the quill in order to tell you that we have safely arrived, Georget and I, and that our mother's donkey suffered no harm, although it caused us a good deal of trouble; for it threw our brother and my baggage into a ditch; but our brother was not resentful at all, and nothing was hurt; and because we arrived too late, Georget sleeps here, and tomorrow morning he will return. O my brother! if only you could see all the tumult, all the hullabaloo and activity, and how happy everyone here seems! you would be completely surprised; for everyone here is a good person, and half of them do not do a thing; one plays, one diverts oneself, one drinks, and all the cabarets are completely packed. We saw all this because the good M. Parangon told us to stroll about in the city for a bit, and one of his apprentices took us all around. Ah! how beautiful the Churches are! If only you could see them! In the Cathedral there is a Saint Christopher who has an oaken walking stick fifty feet long and which only comes up to his chin: oh! it is curious to see! And then there is a very high clock, very high; and on the dial there is a ball that tells the phases of the moon; when it is not there, the moon is new; and when it begins, the ball becomes a bit golden, and then a bit more, and then a bit more, until it is full, whereat it is totally golden; and then it diminishes, it diminishes until it becomes all black again: and then there are promenades planted with trees, which are like the linden tree that is in front of the Church back home; and then there is a river, and then the boats, and then the coaches, and then the floating convoys of wood, and then the mills: I cannot tell you all that there is...[2] what I will tell you is that when I was writing my two other pages, a Demoiselle, whom I mistook for Madame Parangon at first (for unfortunately that Lady is not here, and I did not know it), this Demoiselle then came to look over my shoulder, and she began to laugh, saying: "And then there is this, and then that, and then there is his donkey who plays a part!" She whispered I don't know what into M. Parangon's ear, who came over to read my Letter, and who laughed, and who told me that he would teach me how to write better than that: but I refused to get upset although I felt very embarrassed; for I am quite aware that I write badly, never having written by myself; for when I wrote my Latin lessons, M. le Curate dictated them to me, and never let me do anything on my own. But I finished in short order, lest that laughing head should come back again to look; for I hear M. Parangon saying to her: "His letter is naïve, but it is not so bad." I am, my dear brother, your very humble and very obedient servant and brother,

– Edmond R***.

Give my respects to our father and mother, and my compliments to our brothers and sisters, as well as to Marie-Jeanne.

---

[2]Original footnote: These ellipses are not in the original; I put them everywhere that good sense required them, with all the more freedom given that Edmond, when he had grown up a bit, used them himself. (Copyeditor's note)

II.

December 1ˢᵗ.

THE SAME TO THE SAME.

*Edmond grows tired of the city; he compares his stay
there to that of the countryside.*

My dear brother, I write to you before you have had a
chance to respond to me, and it is in order to assuage
myself, and to tell you that your fate is quite different
from mine, and that I envy you, although I get an education here that I would not get at home; for as I have
some time on my hands, and because I don't know
anything, I have taken to reading a great deal in M.
Parangon's library, where I have found books that I
never heard of before. For instance, the Works of
Boileau, the Comedies of Molière, and also the
Tragedies of Racine and Corneille. I have read these
books with such great pleasure, for they took my
mind off all the annoyances I feel here. In the
evenings, after supper, as it is not good to go outside,
and I don't know anyone, I take a book and I read it
out loud to the cook, who appears to take a great interest in the Tragedies, principally those by the author
Racine; one of those Tragedies, entitled *Berenice*,
made her cry a great deal and me too, recently. But
these amusements cannot last the entire day, and there
are some very hard moments. Ah! my Pierre! You
live satisfied in the place where we were born; you
are free; you do not furrow your brow: your work requires only strong arms and courage; but me, obliged
to concentrate all my attention in order to seize the
principles of a difficult art, I have lost all contentment

and freedom. I have become like a slave; vilified, put off to the side in a strange house, I am given less attention than one of those useless animals that one feeds in order to be amused. Pierrot! O my brother! What a state I am in! And what is it that has brought me to this point? You remember when we were at school under Master Jacques, and I had the misfortune of learning how to read, write, and apply myself more quickly than you did; I always had a quill in hand, I copied the hymns and antiphons that are sung at Church; and because of this, our poor father and mother (with good intentions albeit) thought I was made to become a Doctor; they sent me to M. the Curate to learn Latin; and when they saw that I could read a book in Latin as easily as in French, they were not satisfied, and they determined that I should become an inhabitant of the city in order to make my fortune and one day become the support of our sisters and younger brothers; and then, in order to effect this, that Bailiff unfortunately saw me and recommended that I be placed with M. C***'s son-in-law, and here I am. Oh! the cursed facility that I had then! Eh, what do I care about arriving, as they say, if I must degrade myself first, and mar, by low occupations, the most beautiful days of my life! For here it is not like back home, my dear Pierrot, where everyone lends a hand in the work; my mother, my sisters perform the same tasks as the domestics; my father and you and I, and the plough-hands, we are all one; But here, there are tasks that the master never does, which are considered shameful, and which every honest person holds repugnant, in the opinion of those who expect others to do them; and I am made to do these things, although I am a pupil and not a domestic, because they see that I am amenable and easy-going and not proud like other fellows. I eat my meals in the kitchen; they say that this will last so long as I continue to possess my rustic manners and am not better dressed. What is so wrong with these manners? Or with not being dressed every day in my Sunday best? But these clothes are out of fashion here. In addition to their vices, these people make the mistake of looking down on those who do not resemble them; there is no getting around it. As for myself, I am timid, awkward, as they say; my companions here are, they are impudent, and that is found acceptable here; they praise what at home we find fault with, and they find fault with what any honest person has always praised... But maybe it is a good thing that they keep me at a bit of a distance from them. If you could see how sensual and gluttonous they are at the master's table! Each person consumes as much meat as three of our own people; one could almost say that people in the city live only to eat; it is really a bad example! And if you heard what they say! if you saw the liberties they take with the poor girls who have left their good parents and their poor villages back home, where everyone is treated equally, in order to come to the city and spend their fine days in servitude and contempt! These are such hard words, such scornful comparisons! But it would seem that these poor girls (who are just like us village people) were of a species beneath humanity, that one should have no more modesty dealing with them than with animals. I shut my eyes to all these poverties, for I feel too much shame for them. And what?! If your Marie-Jeanne, that lovely girl, so sweet and modest, worked in the city, a rascal would demand vile services of her, would speak to her in a certain tone of voice, would tell her, would make her, do such things as I see every day inflicted on a young and good domestic girl here!... O my brother! How different things are at home! Everyone is seated round the same table; workhands amongst us brothers; permanent and day-labor handmaids sit beside our sisters; everyone is served without distinction; they are helpers and not servants; our good father presides at the head of the table; that wise old man has the pleasure of seeing his eight girls and five boys (for, alas! I am no longer counted) the most modest and most responsive at the table; he sees the strangers and regards them with the same tenderness that he regards his own children; he listens attentively and respects their instructive and amusing conversation; our good mother, during all this time, ensures that nothing is lacking at the meal, and that everyone is content; and when she has seen to everything, she too listens, and more attentively than anyone.

And then, if you saw also how the peasants are treated who come each week to market to bring them the commodities they need! They are treated with an inconceivable contempt, which seems to me to show the stupidity of these city people; but these poor villagers detest them, and avenge themselves on them for their bad manners by selling to them at the highest possible price, swindling in whatever manner they can those who scorn them; and I believe they find some joy in this small compensation; for without it, I am almost sure that they would not return to do business with them.

Far, then, from seeking out the company of these people here, I hope to avoid their dangerous company as much as possible. Everything about them displeases me; I am bored, my poor brother; I am ill at ease, and I find myself in a situation that I have never been in before; without the books, I could not stand it. When giving my respects to our dear father and mother, tell them that I could quite easily fall ill... No, don't tell them that; for they would grow anxious perhaps and that would be something I would re-proach myself for. Give my best to my brothers and sisters; tell *Ursule,* above all, not to forget me. I salute you with all my heart, and be sure to give my compliments to your dear Marie-Jeanne.

– Your brother and friend, etc.

P.S. M. Parangon showed me a little how one must write; you can see that I have tried to profit by the lesson; but he is quite strict, as to both the form and the content; and as for the young lady who mocked me before, she continues to mock me still.[3]

III.

PIERROT TO EDMOND.

I encourage my brother.[4]

---

[3]Original footnote: We have suppressed all the usual compli-ments, as well as the signatures. (Editor's note)

[4]Original footnote: These Letters' *arguments* are all Pierre R***'s and are found written in his hand on the back of the originals. (Editor's note)

My dear brother, I write these lines to let you know that I received your letter, on the first of the current; and, at the same time, in order to tell you that we are delighted to receive your news; and that since you left S***, we no longer have any fun; and that my mother cries every day, no longer to be able to see you; and your brothers and sisters and I, it feels like it has been ten years since we last saw you. But we must all take heart, my poor Edmond, for as they say, there are no beginnings without sacrifices; and as for what concerns us all, we wished you were here; but our father says that it is not to your benefit, and that consoles us a little that you are no longer with us; and as for those city people, you must not let that surprise you or cause you grief. Be patient; for when you know your profession as a Painter, you will no longer depend on anyone. It is a fine and good profession, despite the proverb, when one is skilled at it. Your master is rich, and all the Lords of manor in the area want to employ him; and he said as much to our good father when he spoke to him in V***, that a Painter from Portugal, whose name is Avelar, had bought all the buildings on one entire street in the city of Lisbon, which is a kind of Paris; and that that Painter had changed the proverb, for in the city of Lisbon one said, "Rich like the Painter Avelar"; and it is only the debauched who are poor and miserable; but you are not like that, my Edmond, nor inclined to be, thank God. Keep well; be happy, and come visit us during the Noel festivities. Ursule and all us brothers and sisters send you our best wishes, and Marie-Jeanne does too: she thanks you for thinking of her.

Our good mother embraces you; she said so

this morning in her own words: "Remind him to fear the good God, to take care of himself, and he will lack nothing." Don't worry about what you write; for you know that it will always be me who fetches your Letters from the post office when going to the market in V***, and that I will show only what is appropriate to show.

IV.

Edmond to Pierrot.

How he was mistreated; he begins speaking with Mademoiselle Tiennete.

My disgust for the city has only augmented, dear brother, since the time that I have been here, and I need to remember everything that our good father told me during Christmas holidays so as not to become completely discouraged. Melancholy wears me down, and if it weren't for the hope that I have to see you during Easter holidays, I would have a worse time of it, I fear. I have just asked for permission to depart on Holy Saturday at noon, and my request has been granted; but if it hadn't been for a person who is here, I would not have had that satisfaction. For you already know, my brother, that during the absence of Madame Parangon, who is in Paris, one of her relatives stands in for her, and manages the household; she's a tall girl, well-made, quite pretty, but so haughty, so vain, so impertinent, so full of herself, that whenever her eye falls on you she seems to demand adoration. Mademoiselle Manon Palestine (that's how she is called), from the very first day, has taken it into her head to employ me in tasks that have very little to do with my profession, because I have a good nature (as I have already noted and said); I made myself available and would perhaps have rendered her even more menial services (for I do not know how to refuse anyone, and above all a pretty girl: the pleasure surpasses the pain, if to be obeyed she employs nothing but the rights of her beauty). And as people quickly grow accustomed to the sweet feeling of giving orders, I have become necessary to her. And that is why she opposes my departure. The master responded that, given that my certificate of apprenticeship[5] had not yet been awarded, I was free to go, and that besides, it was good for me to spend some time with my parents, to let them know how I was getting along in my new position. After my request had been granted, she had nothing but negative things to say to me; she is the first woman to make me realize that it is not enough to be pretty to likable. Yesterday, for example, I gave her a cake as a present; she gave it to the old pupils, pretending to pay no attention to me. I am not one to enjoy eating cake all that much; but, my brother, people just don't act like that where we come from; one would be afraid to mortify, by the least slight, someone like Blaisot, the little shepherd. That Mademoiselle Manon!... I find her cruel!... She humiliates everyone (who displeases her, of course): if you saw how she treats the servant girl of the house! I am ashamed for her sometimes. Mademoi-

---

[5]Original footnote: This word *certificate* [*brevet* in French] should not cause any surprise; Painters who are established in the countryside draw different services from their students and have them commit to a multi-year engagement. (Editor's note)

selle thinks it is beneath her dignity to use her own hands; it is always, "Tiennete, give me this; Tiennete, give me that." If Tiennete does not promptly respond, she is a beast, a sot, an imbecile, a cretin, and the like. I believe that the poor Tiennete's biggest mistake is to be as young and pretty as Mademoiselle Manon is, if not more so. Is it possible (and I often ask myself) for someone to be so disrespectful to one's similars! Honestly, I would not have believed it if I had not seen it with my own two eyes.

So I will leave at noon on Easter eve; I will go quickly; come out to meet me as far as the Courtenai woods or even Provenchère, so that I might have the pleasure of embracing you a few moments earlier. Give my respects to our dear father and mother. I am thinking of what Ursule said to me; show her this line, but only in private, lest it cause any jealousy. Looking forward to seeing you, my friend.

V.

THE SAME TO THE SAME.

Good feelings, which did not last long enough.

In order to feel the joy of having parents such as ours, I needed to have separated from them for a while, dear older brother. How touched I am! Since my return, I cannot help reminding myself of the good advice they gave me, or remembering the affection they showed me... that all of you showed me. I am stronger for having seen them, and for their having taught me a thousand things about the perversity of men, whom they assured me (and I truly believe it) that it would have been more harmful than beneficial to instruct me about before I moved to the city. Nor do I forget what you told me, you primarily, my Pierre, and the dear Ursule. There is not a single family here that is united like ours; we are fourteen children, and there is not a single one of us who would not sacrifice himself for the others. We will not be rich, but we will love each other: the portion of the paternal estate that we will mutually come away with is not worth a thousandth part of the treasure of friendship that each of us has for the other, brothers and sisters. Take heart, my Pierre; the more advanced in age will assist the younger; we will all support each other like the children of that old man whose story I read the other day: he made them take a bundle of small sticks, not unlike our bunch of twigs, and he told them to snap them; nobody could do it; then he took each one singly, he who was old and dying, and snapped it, one after the other: a good lesson for us! Our unity, and the happiness we procure from it, is our good mother's sweetest hope; we would truly be ungrateful not to give her that satisfaction. I think however that our dear father and mother's intentions would have been better fulfilled if they had made us all work in the fields; a family such as our own would have been the equal of an entire hamlet; we would have improved the already cultivated legacy, and we would have enriched our father in the most honorable way, for him and for ourselves. What am I trying to say, my Pierre? They would have given me Laurote, our little cousin from mother's side of the family, just as they will give you Marie-Jeanne... But all that is not, and never will be, in the cards for me; I must no longer think about it.

I am still quite at odds with Mademoiselle Manon; she enjoys ridiculing me, humiliating me in everything. I forgive her however; Tiennete has set the example for me. One day, when that girl had been roundly scolded, I heard what she said to Mademoiselle Manon:

"You are my mistress, and more enlightened than me; I think that everything you tell me is for my own good; I am much obliged to you, and I love you all the more for it."

I was surprised by these sentiments in a village girl who is not even eighteen years old, and who was speaking to a young person just like herself; I could not help feeling bad that a person who appears so well-born, and who comes from a good family, could resolve to degrade herself by servitude. But one must profit from examples of virtue, from whatever quarter they come. That response, I believe, made an impression on Mademoiselle Manon; Tiennete is better treated now, and me worse. That natural pride, which human qualities must inspire in us, I cannot help letting her see it, and that revolts Mademoiselle Manon; which surprises me a little less, since I notice that city people, not prizing what they call the beautiful sex as much as we do, show it much more deference however. But their true dispositions show through when they find themselves around women over whom they have a superiority of wealth; they compensate themselves then, with interest, for all the humiliations they are forced to undergo before their equals.

I find it enjoyable conversing with Tiennete: this young lady is Sweetness itself; she has common sense, and a great fund of virtue. I'm told that she would need it in order to resist the attacks of my master. M. Loiseau, from her same village, is the one who made these reflections. I could not believe my ears. A married man with so charming a wife (for well do I remember now having seen her in V***, when we were at M. her father's house in order to introduce myself, our parents and I), to forget his duties in such a way!... it is beyond me. He is also (and I say this to you in confidence) a Freemason, one of those people who see the devil in their assemblies, under the guise of a big black bull.[6] But one sees many other things of that sort here... To return to Tiennete, this young lady is modest; she does not like to be pursued; I am the only person in the household whose assiduity she enjoys because I am careful in what I say, because I take great pleasure in the company of her fellow villager M. Loiseau, and because when we are together, out of kindness, I make an effort to read aloud while she is doing her work. She is very sensitive: yesterday, after supper, I was reading a book to her, wherein there was the letter by a certain Ariadne to a traitor named Theseus who had abandoned her on a deserted island; as I was reading, I lifted my eyes and I could see her all in tears. O my God! How lovely she looked like that... but she serves. She reminds me of Marie-Jeanne sometimes; your lovely mistress is of the same character as Tiennete. You must be so happy!... If

____

[6]Original footnote: A popular prejudice in the countryside.

Laurote were not so young, do you think she would be the equal of Marie-Jeanne? But don't tell me about it.

I write to you about this and that, and I stop when I have nothing more to say. Good evening, my Pierre; always love,

– Your faithful Edmond.

VI.

May 26, Feast Day of S. Pélerin.

PIERROT TO EDMOND.

My feelings on servitude in the city.

This letter, my Edmond, is in response to yours, which gives me a great deal to think about; it's what makes me hesitate to show it to our father, or even to our mother; for you know how sensitive they are about honor; and your frequentation with Tiennete would not please them; and you know very well that they are opposed to the feelings that you are beginning to have for our cousin Laurote; and because she is from the country, and you need to establish yourself in the city, they would be all the more opposed to your feelings if you were to fall enamored with a servant; and far be it from me to disdain anyone, as you well know; but when a girl has been a servant in the city, you know, my Edmond, that marks her in a certain way: my father and mother have said as much a hundred times; and so, as you yourself have pointed out to me in one of your letters, a good plough-hand, a harvester from these parts, a girl that is employed to help keep the house, have nothing to be reproached for; for they are like children of the same family; but, son of a gun! a servant in the city, a lackey in livery, all those who do low things or who suffer because of it, that is repugnant, Edmond, that is repugnant; for people with a good heart never lower themselves to that degree. I feel for that poor girl, for what it's worth, and one ought to show her some courtesy; but not too much companionship. Mademoiselle Manon is a funny girl; but what is all that presumptuousness to you? When Madame Parangon returns, you won't have any more to do with that fashionista, who thinks that she is descended from St. Louis' rib, but who comes from the same stock that we do through the Quatrevaux de Saint-Cyr, who come from the Nitri, and who, throughout time, are connected with our family. We are merely a quarter relation and already one fails to recognize us! But what has that got to do with us? As far as Ursule is concerned, she complains that you have forgotten her: know that she is the only one among us who has seen your Letter, with Marie-Jeanne, from whom I concealed the ending. All three of us embrace you.

VII.

June 24, Feast Day of St. John.

EDMOND TO PIERROT.

Dangerous example.

I do not believe, my brother, that anything I said justifies the fears you express; I take them for a new proof of your affection; but rest assured, Tiennete is not dangerous, not for me at any rate; that lovely girl has deemed me worthy of her confidence. She loves, and she is loved; a rash step, which I do not approve, has placed her in a situation that she's not suited for. I will reveal to you her secret, because I know that I can trust you with it. Her family is from the city of Aval***, where they are respected; Tiennete left her parents' home on account of someone whom they wanted her to marry, despite the repugnance she demonstrated; they do not know where she is, as you might imagine. Her lover followed her, but without putting Mademoiselle Tiennete's reputation at risk; from before the time when his mistress ran away, he had begged his mother and father to place him with a Solicitor in the city, to allow him a better opportunity to watch over her; and he arrived two weeks after she did. These poor lovers see each other every day after supper, in my presence: previously, Tiennete forwent these encounters; but since our friendship, we exit together in the evening, under the pretext of taking a bit of fresh air, and we wend our way to the place St. Etienne where M. Loiseau joins us. Tiennete and he say sweet things to each other, which softens my heart, and it seems to me that I am partially a participant in their affection; I am also quite happy to assist them; for their frequentation is honest, and they do not say anything that their parents could not hear. For example, without me Tiennete today was not planning to go with her lover to the Arquebuse where one hunts for birds; it is a very nice fair that the entire city attends, and above all the Ladies, in very brilliant attire.

As for what you say about our family's quarter relation with Mademoiselle Manon, I do not think she knows about it; but if she did, it would be all the same to her. Here, brothers and sisters barely consider themselves related; and if an uncle has no children and nobody is expected to inherit from him, he is but a stranger to his nieces and nephews. I have even seen married couples who forgot that they had a father, if it wasn't for the custom each year of going to signing his guestbook on January 1ˢᵗ. With that in mind, judge for yourself what she will do with your quarter relation comment.

I charge you with telling our dear father, while assuring him of my deep respect and filial tenderness for him, that M. Parangon expects him next Thursday, to award me my certificate of apprenticeship; because the time of my apprenticeship does not start until that day, I entreat him not to delay. There was some talk of waiting for Madame Parangon to return, but she has not yet finished the business that detains her; so he will award it to me anyways, according to his desire.

Give all our brothers and sisters a big hug for me. Tell Ursule that she is wrong to complain, and that she is always present in my thoughts; I am always and forever, for her as well as for you, the most affectionate of brothers.

VIII.

August 15, Feast Day of the Virgin.

THE SAME TO THE SAME.

One begins to flatter him, and he likes it.

Now that my certificate of apprenticeship has been awarded, Mademoiselle Manon begins to show me some of her human qualities; she deigns to speak with me, and sometimes she smiles at me. Despite the knowledge I have of her character, I feel only too inclined to forget all the ill, in order to see only the good: I find her prettier with each passing day. Back home, the girls have only the beauty of their face and waist; those who are ugly seem so completely; those who are kind seem so only partially: but in the city, their charms are multiplied; without mentioning an appetizing whiteness of the skin, which is almost never found in the countryside, the girls here profit by the beauty of their hair and all the rest. I have never heard anyone praise the beauty of someone's hands in our village; here a beautiful hand has its virtue. A pretty foot, hidden in a wooden sabot or a coarse shoe, – nobody notices it there; here, everything is utilized to bring out the best advantages of that appendage, and that of a pretty leg. I almost don't dare tell you how little of a dazzling bosom is left to the imagination; that the women squeeze themselves into their dresses to the point of suffocation, in order to have a thinner waist; that they employ small affectations, small coquetries, and small mannerisms, mere glances from below, capable of disconcerting the most confident of men. The women back home all look the same; here in the city, everyone knows how to employ whatever they have to their advantage; even an ugly girl knows how to dress and how to prepare her toilette so as make herself look passable, so that at the beginning of my stay here I concluded that all the women were pretty; and it was only after a while that I began to discern differences.

To return to the subject of Mademoiselle Manon, she told Tiennete that I was beginning to develop, and that I would make a handsome young man one day. Finally, she asked her a thousand adroit questions in order to understand whether I spoke about her. Tiennete said that I did not, and that I was a very decent young man, who spent all my free time reading. Mademoiselle Manon replied that that was good to hear, and that I was wrong to believe that she did not like me.

"O my God, Mademoiselle," Tiennete said, "that is not at all what he thinks. If he speaks of you, he says only good things: did someone say that he spoke poorly of you?"

"No, no,... only, I find him too timid;... one might say that he was afraid of me... Tell him that if he spoke to me, I will not eat him alive."

Tiennete did not fail to report all this to me.

In the afternoon, Mademoiselle Manon was alone in the room when I came down to work in the atelier. She came over to see my drawings; because she is learning herself, and because she is much more advanced than I am, she was kind enough to give me some advice. There is nothing that has so much power over my heart as sweet words and good manners. I was completely beside myself when, by chance, her foot pressed up against mine: it only lasted but a second; she blushed, saying to me: "Did I hurt you?" I did not respond; but I would have wished to say: "No, Mademoiselle, I rather enjoyed it." Then we chatted a bit. Mademoiselle Manon told me that when I first came from my village, she did not find my appearance to be as good as she does now; that my gawky attitude made me look silly; that she was pleased to admit that she had been mistaken. "Your city finery," she added, "that beautiful hair of yours which you no longer neglect, the ease you have acquired, all make you look like a totally different person, and give you... an air... but a... seductive air. Your thick and arched eyebrows give a certain vivacity to your big eyes,... which, however, still express only timidity; your aquiline nose is a little long, but it does no harm; but those lips! I have never seen lips before that were... so red; what freshness! (She touched them with her finger, and my face immediately turned red like the lips she was praising; she smiled so pleasantly!... as the girls back home never smile, my dear Pierrot). "You are well made," she continued, "although you have not yet reached your full height... When you first arrived," she continued again, "who would have guessed that your leg was so fine, under your mud-splattered leggings?... Edmond, believe me, one day you will be a handsome knight." Oh, Pierre! I would never have imagined her to be so fine! What joy she gave me! At home, one does not know what to say to any of these things; and even though we make it known that we esteem each other, and that such things are said sometimes, we never praise each other. I begin to realize that shortcomings are everywhere compensated by qualities, and bad by good. I was far from growing tired of Mademoiselle Manon, who had just placed her hand on mine, when M. Parangon appeared. She pulled it back quickly; but he had seen her; he looked at us with a somber and withering look, telling me to go and work in our atelier.

I begin to grow accustomed to the city; everything that had previously displeased me need only be seen from a certain angle: but I think however that if the girls of our village had a bit of the art of those of the city, we would be much happier at home. I am all in favor of placing our Ursule in apprenticeship here, as she desires, and as we have spoken about: she is pretty, and I think that when she has acquired the manners and what is called in high society the graces, she would surpass the young ladies who pass for the best in the city of Au***, and that she could find a situation here incomparably more advantageous than in S***. Encourage our dear father and mother about it: I am doubly interested, both because it is to my sister's advantage, and because she would make an agreeable companion for me here, which would allow me to avoid falling into bad company. I am, in anticipation of your pleasant news, your best friend, etc.

IX.

M. Parangon to Father d'Arras, Cordelier.[7]

He proposes to deceive Edmond, and Father d'Arras begins to play a part.

---

[7]Cordelier: an Observant, or Conventual, Franciscan.

I entreat you, my father, to receive among the number of your practicants a young man from the country who has been a pupil of mine for the last seven or eight months. I have my reasons for putting him in such good hands as yours. He is simple and correct without being foolish: I have plans that I am in a hurry to complete, while he still possesses his rustic naïvety; I am somewhat familiar with these types; a person is the master of them while they are still in a formative stage, but if you wait for them to wise up, they are a hundred times worse than our city youth; when they emerge from their ignorance and become enlightened, they understand both evil and good, so they leave you without any hope of return. Besides, what I wish to do for him (except for the *retentum*, which he will never know about) is a real advantage, which I am sure will fill his father, who is a good man, and his mother, a very good woman, with joy; they are burthened with a large family; consequently, their children will not be rich; a good dowry will flatter them. Without that, I am too honest to abuse the confidence that they place in me, those who give me their children for pupils. I remain, with the assurance that you will second me, dear Father,

Yours, etc.

X.

RESPONSE.

How he plans to take control of Edmond's mind.

The pretty cousin had already informed me: I accept;

send him here tomorrow morning at eight o'clock; your little country boy will be quite recalcitrant if I cannot succeed with him.

The manner in which, as the amiable cousin tells me, you have dealt with him is very philosophical, and shows that you two have a perfect knowledge of the human heart. What to do then! I could not have done any better myself. You demean him, you make him eat in the kitchen, so that he naturally considers himself far beneath you: Manon put him off, mortified him, so that he might all the more keenly feel the value of her kindness when she shows it! My faith, for a girl of nineteen, that's some understanding! and the young man has from now on good reason to believe that she has more wit, sense, and maturity than old people of yesteryear. I will second you, but you give me a mediocre task; it is you who will have done everything.

I have just received the portrait. I find that you have embellished the little person, and that you have painted her precisely as she believes herself to be: it is a new sign of your superior talent; you see by the attitude that the sitter takes, by the physiognomy that she wishes to have. Your two small paintings are delicious; it is a gift that I have imagined our Guardian wanted to make, and that I will make to him myself, knowing how much I oblige him thereby: I will tell you all about it when we see each other (and that will be soon; for my service ends on Sunday). A Lady who examines them while I write would desire for a certain part that something that you know; I observe that all women have this predilection, even in painting; it happens quite often however that one finds this *something* in real life. The inviolable secrecy surrounding these paintings and the portrait; she for whom they are destined: cannot permit that they be seen, or that the honor of such beautiful work be attributed to you, so long as the hand from whom they come remains a mystery: she has a mother who is complacency itself; everything that is given, it is a gift by the mother; they both profit by it; the husband cherishes so good a mother and renders her what the suitors have given to the daughter, so the gift is double. One thing that should flatter you is that M. Gaudet likes your miniatures so much that he wants to multiply them by his engravery.

Farewell, Parangon: never spare me, even indirectly, in anything that concerns you; it is always a pleasure to render you a service, when you furnish me the opportunity to do so.

P.S. And that dear other half of yours, when will she return? She is an angel; but she is also a woman, I see it in her preference for the Capital.

XI.

August 29, our parish feast day.

PIERROT TO EDMOND.

I give my advice like a man without experience.

Today is a day we would have all been most desirous of your presence, my dear brother. At dinner, my father had us all gather round him and gave us his benediction, and double for me so that I might give you yours, as by the present letter I pass it on to you with all my heart, my dear Edmond: and then our mother gave us all a piece of cake; and our father said to her: "Woman that you are, is your son then among the wolves and among assassins that you are crying for him? Come on, have some courage! one must let one's children go, for their own good; and I plan also to send Ursule to the city." And our good mother went into kitchen where she had a good cry before drying her eyes; but for the rest of the day they were red. I need to tell you that your letter took a load off my mind: I was afraid, despite what you told me, that that Tiennete might catch your eye, and that you might fall in love with her. Whatever her intent is, she is a servant in the city, and she has aggrieved her mother and father, who do not know what has become of her, and that is not at all good. But Mademoiselle Manon, she's different! and her friendship, if she takes kindly to you, could lead you far. Who knows?... I showed your letter to our mother this afternoon, and it set her mind a little at ease; and she said that she would love a lovely daughter-in-law like her; for she has seen Mademoiselle Manon in V***, when you visited there with our good mother and father. But you need to behave, and not be too free; you know quite well that M. Parangon would not like that. I cannot write any more than this, my Edmond, despite the pleasure it gives me; for I have the barley to stack up, and the rye seed to prepare, which we will sow in the coming days. Goodbye my friend; always keep me abreast of every little thing; it keeps me from boredom in your absence. The entire family embraces you with all their heart; but Ursule and I, as well as Marie-Jeanne, a bit more affectionately still.

XII.

Sunday, September 1.

Response.

One sees by this that the city has already changed him quite a bit. He begins to speak about Mademoiselle Edmée.

Your letter gave me so much pleasure, my brother. I showed part of it to Tiennete; she wept warm tears before she saw any mention of herself; but when she saw it, she wept even harder; she told me that she hoped one day to regain the estimation of so honest a young man as yourself. That's quite sweet, my Pierre! And what you said is quite harsh!... But it is for a good reason, and Tiennete herself approves of you, in that respect. Let's speak about something else.

At this moment, I am losing myself in the *mores* of the city (*mores:* in other words, the usages, conduct, ways of acting): Who would have thought?... O my brother, you are the only person to whom I wish to reveal this mystery... I don't know where to begin... Yesterday, M. Parangon, and Mademoiselle Manon... Oh! it's really quite bad! I would not have thought that Mademoiselle Manon... In short, yesterday, I was going to look for something I needed from the room above Madame Parangon's room: her room is always locked; but I thought I heard Mademoiselle

Manon's voice inside as I passed; a certain tendency that I have found in myself when she is around, made me approach, and I put my ear to the door. I was quite taken aback when I heard M. Parangon's voice too. I was going to withdraw, but something strange prevented me; it was as if he had embraced her. I could not resist the temptation of looking through the keyhole; and I saw, yes, my dear brother, I saw my master holding a young woman in his arms, whose face I did not see, but who could not have been anyone else than his wife's cousin, for I had just heard her voice. Whoever it was, she was wearing a dress that I hadn't seen Mademoiselle Manon wear before during the day. At first, she seemed to resist him; I heard her saying, but very softly, and in a voice that I could not quite make out, that Madame Parangon was going to return soon and that they should begin behaving themselves. (*Begin*, I said to myself!) M. Parangon showed no signs of abating, just the opposite; and as they moved, I could no longer see anything; but all I could hear was whoever it was, defending herself.

I withdrew. I was completely I don't know what. I went downstairs to the hall: I wanted to apply myself to drawing: what I did was of no consequence; I went into the garden to walk it off; everything displeased me; I passed Tiennete in the kitchen who was returning, and who seemed overheated. I was so discountenanced that she noticed it; she asked me what was wrong. I replied, a bit sullenly, "Nothing." – "You're upset at least?"[8] – "Ah! Tiennete!" – "A sigh!" – "Me, sigh!" – "Would you be blushing?" –

---

[8]Original footnote: I add these dashes – instead of *she said, I responded*, etc. in the original. (Editor's note)

"Yes, I would be, if..." – "But you are quite worked up, Monsieur?... some rebuffs, perhaps?... Edmund! what is all that compared to what I suffer!" – "But it is nothing." – "Come on, what Mademoiselle Manon does to you weighs on your heart: but there is someone who knows about it, and who will make all that stop." – "Little does it matter, if what I saw..."

Tiennete did not understand; Mademoiselle Manon called her, and I exited. That girl is prudence itself; she knows more than she lets on, certainly; but she does not say a thing; she does not wish to speak ill of someone or to penetrate others' secrets... And now Mademoiselle Manon is calling me too. I will stop here for today; tomorrow, I will pick it up again.

The continuation.

June 24, St. John's Day.

I continue my confession to you, my Pierre. Mademoiselle Manon is quite deceitful! (Supposing that it was she who was with M. Parangon, as I recounted to you yesterday.) Would you believe that she acted one hundred times more friendly with me than ever? She is so brazen! It is true that she does not know to question whether I have suspicions, or whether I saw or heard anything; but she knows what she did; and I think that a young lady like that (if she is culpable; for one can be mistaken) ought to fear that one might read in her eyes what she has in her soul, and to see in those of others the reproaches that she merits: at least, this is what I would fear if I were her. But, blast it! it is the furthest thing from her thoughts! These are merely cajoleries and considerations. Oh! If I did not doubt her!... hmm! the wicked person! (if it was she): one must have the honor to resist! I'm grateful to be able to tell you everything; it will serve me well in the end, if I was tempted to be so craven as to love a girl who is not good (if it was she, you understand). She told me just now that M. Parangon plans to accompany her soon to a fair,[9] in a hamlet at one league from the city, named Saint-loup-en-Vaux, where everyone goes today to divert themselves: she added that I could go there, look for them, and join them, as if I had run into them by chance. I plan to do nothing of the sort. But I will go to the fair, however; Tiennete begged me to take her there so that M. Loiseau might run into her, without her violating her strict rules of behavior. We prepare to depart now, I will finish my letter this evening.

10 o'clock in the evening.

Oh! I have so many things to tell you, my Pierre. We just came back from the fair: I have never seen such a good fair. Imagine an entire city, important people and little people enjoying themselves in the country-side. As I said, Vaux is one league from the city; it's on the edge of the river that flows to the north, at the end of a beautiful prairie; one cannot reach it except by descending on foot because of a hill at the edge of the city, which is too steep; a strong river runs in the

---

[9]Original footnote: They are called small fairs, and they are like those in the parishes of Paris where one goes to have a good time, to dance, etc.

middle of it, which leaves from the foot of the neigh-
boring hillsides; its edges are lined by willow trees
and poplars, which gives it the most agreeable shade
one could imagine. There one finds, on one side, the
regular or country dances; on the other, tables where
joy reigns, and all sorts of games. This spectacle, new
for me, intoxicated me in a way: I just stood there
looking for a time, as if my soul were in my eyes. To
extract me from my ecstasy, M. Loiseau pointed out
to me Mademoiselle Manon who was dancing; I hid
myself in the crowd, in order to watch her without being seen. Oh, Pierre! How is it possible that a liar, a...
(supposing that what I saw was real, and that it was
she who was in the room), how is it possible that a
girl of this caliber could have so many graces, and
that she could seduce everyone!... And look at all the
men whose heads turn!... I think that after she finished dancing I would have joined her, as she had
asked me to, if I had not heard the sound of a hautboy
behind me: I turned; I saw a group of young female
wine workers from the city who were going to dance
a round. Tiennete and Loiseau ran forward and led me
along with them. These girls did not want to allow the
boys to follow them, to dance with them; one, primarily, more opinionated than the others, was absolutely
opposed to it, saying that they were drunk. She interested me, I drew near in order to see her close up. No,
it is not possible to imagine anyone prettier: Albano[10]
could not have imagined sweeter eyes; the divine
Raphael could not have painted a more perfect head;

---

[10]Albano: Francesco Albani (AD 1578-1660), an Italian painter
from Bologna.

Veronese[11] could not have matched the violets and roses in her beautiful cheeks; and yet they are the greatest painters. She goes by the name of Edmée: she is a piquant brunette (as they say here), about seventeen years old, as timid as the girls back home; lively, as cheerful with her companions as anyone in the city; with a gentleness in her looks, with her embarrassment when a young man speaks to her, with a lovely blush in her cheeks, which will not last. I had an inordinate desire to grab her hand away from that rustic who had coarsely seized it. These peasants from the city have a certain rusticity of the fields in their manner, combined with the free attitudes of the city, which makes them completely repellant; back home, at least, modesty and restraint conceal a portion of their coarseness; the boldness of these people here however is put on full display, and they glory in it. Tiennete joined in with these girls; her costume, just like theirs almost, made her fit in; then, she knew how to dance with them with such address that they allowed M. Loiseau and me to join in their round dance. I managed to position myself beside the pretty brunette; I read in her eyes that she was planning to change places, and I made an effort to keep her, by employing the most polite expressions. I would have failed in my efforts if it weren't for Edmée's sister who heard me and chimed in, saying to her: "O my Lord God, Edmée, this Gentleman is not going to eat you! And when you stop with the pretensions, it will just make things better." The charming Edmée lowered her gaze, and she let me take her hand without

---

[11]Veronese: Bonifacio Veronese (AD 1487-1553), an Italian painter from the Venetian Republic.

resistance. Soon the dance grew animated, and that succeeded in bringing her cheerfulness out, which seemed to be at the core of Edmée's character; it came out in spite of her. Then we danced the hop, and I had the pleasure... oh, what a pleasure!... to hold her in my arms. Tiennete, in gratitude for the complaisance that the girls had in allowing us to join them, encouraged them to have a bite to eat with us. They all accepted very graciously; but we had a real difficulty trying to convince Edmée; she would not relent in spite of what her sister said, a very attractive, chubby girl, who willingly accepted. I have never had a more enjoyable meal in my life. I noticed that too much forwardness displeased Edmée; I dealt with her short humor, or, as they say here, her touchy delicatesse, by sharing my attention with all her companions; but, on the sly, I studied her eyes to divine what pleased her, and I treated her to a kind of nonchalance and distraction; which had its effect; for she came out of her shell when she thought that I had no preference for her. After the meal, Tiennete and Loiseau entertained them with a *bourguignote*, a simple and lively dance, which most people in Au*** are unfamiliar with, as well as back home, but which is well-known in Morvand. My faith, the quadrilles of the city, the minuets, the passepieds, the hornpipes, the allemandes are nothing in comparison, when one dances like Tiennete and Loiseau. But we were soon sorry for it; for a crowd gathered around us; M. Parangon and Mademoiselle Manon came with the others: this last person made a sign of noticing me; I could not help but approach her, and I noticed that from then on the young Edmée followed me with her eyes; it's what made me stay on my guard, and act with great reserve, when speaking with Mademoiselle Manon. Fortunately for me, M. Parangon did not look kindly on our conversation; he came over to interrupt it, and Mademoiselle Manon could not hide her vexation; her bad mood was taken out on Tiennete (whom everyone praised for her grace and modesty, although she was dressed like a Morvandaise, but that is what made her look so pretty!...); she asked her who had given her permission to come to the fair. M. Parangon replied for her, that it was him. Mademoiselle Manon bit her lip and turned her back to us. I was delighted by it, as were Tiennete and Loiseau; we hastened to rejoin Edmée and her companions. All those rustics whom we had at first seen around her had returned. I asked Edmée's sister if those fellows had accompanied them to the fair. "We don't need them to accompany us," she said; "we come on our own accord; we know them, for they live on the little rue Saint Germain; but we have never hung out with them." I was glad to hear that. I proposed to Tiennete that we distance ourselves from the crowd and amuse ourselves by playing some games with the girls. We snuck away from those importunate fellows, who had begun to drink copiously; and at a place to the side, the prettiest place in the world, we played at M. the Curate. You know what that is: oh! my Pierre, what a pleasure it gave me! I made a point of not being named the Curate; it was Loiseau who was chosen on my refusal; and Edmée's pretty little mouth had to say the informal "tu" to me. Every time I had to respond, it was she whom I called; between the fear she had of making a pledge, and her timid modesty, which prevented her from addressing me too familiarly, she hesitated, blushed; but how gracefully!... Pierrot, Pierrot! I could not take it... but I still was not chosen. Pledges were given round; as for me, I had put so much into it!... A thousand things were commanded of me; I desired only one: finally my desires were satisfied. It was Edmée's sister's turn to order me: "You have *three choices, choose one: first, fly in the air; second, take the moon with your teeth; third,...* my faith, what else can I come up with... *kiss Edmée.*" I felt almost dizzy on hearing this; as I write this to you now, my heart is still thumping; my whole body was shaking with pleasure as I rose; while taking Edmée by the waist, and pressing my mouth to her cheeks, softer and redder than rose petals, my heart was melting. Ah! what agreeable breath! it is like the *first gentle breezes of spring...*[12] She no longer dared to look at me for the duration of the game. That modesty, my brother, adds much to the charm of her beauty... Oh! the delightful game, the delightful game for love!

But it was growing late; the sun, which was beginning to set, announced the end of so beautiful a day, and the time to return to the city. We departed; but as we reached the summit of the hill, the rustics approached us in order to insult us. I was between Edmée and her sister, whom I had just helped up the hill: one of them came up behind me to give me a blow on the back of the neck. I'm not a quarreler; but whoever looks for me finds me. I had gently let go of Edmée's arm, and I sought the eyes of the brute who had struck me: I did not want to cause him a lot of harm; I seized

---

[12]Original footnote: Zephyrs, or Mediterranean winds.

him firmly; and then, after having shaken him a moment, I threw him down, several feet away from me, on the grass that borders the path; he got up so heavily, and he was so out of balance, that he fell again, and rolled from the top of the hill to the bottom, accompanied by the cries of two thousand people. His companions wanted to avenge him; it is at this moment that I saw the lovable Edmée show an interest in me; she employed, in order to restrain them, the sweetest words with them. I smiled at her fears; but it gave me so much pleasure, so much pleasure!... As these fellows were filled with wine, Loiseau and I had no trouble making them follow, one after the other, the same route as their comrade. We had gotten rid of them in this way, and we tranquilly resumed our way. But can you believe my absent-mindedness! Upon reaching the city, the crowd separated us (and perhaps this was a trick by Edmée's sister; for she had said something to her at around this time), I did not have the foresight to ask them where they lived, to the effect that I have no idea how to find my charming brunette again; even though the city is not immense. Tiennete poked a great deal of fun at me for my inattention, and Loiseau congratulated me on my taste (but he thought I had asked them their address); he found the young lady to be as deserving as she was beautiful. His mistress piled on to these praises, and then the two of them looked at each other... The truth of the matter is that they really love each other!... I already knew as much, but I understand now just how happy they must be, since I have seen Edmée.

XIII.

September 8, Day of the Virgin.

PIERROT TO EDMOND.

I address some remonstrances at him.

This letter is in response to your long letter, my Edmond. After reading the beginning of it, I stood like a stone. O Lord! that Demoiselle Manon! She's a viper that girl (supposing, as you say, that it is she)! And in that case, one should not give her the time of day anymore. I had thought however that there was something there for you; but it could very well have been less than nothing; but one will still need to wait and see before telling her flat out, *abrenuntio Satana*[13] (as they say at baptism). Whatever you say or do, I do not like Tiennete; when a person walks straight, he does not hide; there is something she's not telling you. As for that nice Edmée, whom you speak a lot about, she does not please me as much as Mademoiselle Manon would have, you see, my friend; do not go attaching yourself to someone without really knowing what she is about; one must first see to the bottom of something; that's my advice. In this way, if she is from a good family and if she has aspirations, I will support you; otherwise, *nescio vos*. Don't act too quickly out of need: court her as we do here; people frequent each other for four or five years before hitching up, and one is hardly any more familiar for that; oftentimes, one converses more with the father and mother than with the girl; and that is good; one understands how they run the family, and one profits by their counsel;

---

[13]*Abrenuntio Satana*: Latin for "I renounce [you], Satan."

whereas youth to youth, one speaks only nonsense. I will tell you that there is talk of having us marry, Marie-Jeanne and I, this winter: it is just as our parents want, and hers. I believe that I will have an honest and lovable wife; so I am content. Ursule from time to time speaks to our mother about going to live close to you; but I don't recommend it, until I see you more fixed and more settled. I don't like the story of your fighting in Vaux; that sounds like something a presumptuous person would do; here at home, in a like case, reasonable people talk, and they do not throw someone down a hill: what if you had hurt them, and they had brought you to court!... That's not a big deal; but it attracts attention; here one would say, *Edmond R*** went to fisticuffs with some drunken fellows; he was apparently drunk himself?* It is a matter of honor. But to avoid upsetting you, I will pass along two words to you from our good mother.

> *My Edmond; I am sending silk stockings and culottes to you, two vests and the baracan suit, to make you look well-dressed on Sundays and feast days: my Pierrot tells me everything, and he tells me that a good match presents itself to you, if you are good: you must be, my child. I embrace you with all my heart.*
>
> *– Your Mother, BARBE DE BERTRO.*

I didn't dictate any of that, it is all from her; for you see, my Edmond, that would be lacking in respect, and performing a kind of sacrilege by inserting myself into it. Adieu; love your brother as much as he loves you.

Ursule and Marie-Jeanne send you their best, as does the entire family.

XIV.

EDMOND TO PIERROT.

Villainy on the part of his master: Edmond makes the acquaintance of Father d'Arras.

One must distrust what one hears through a door, and what one sees through a keyhole, dear older brother. That's what master Jacques, our Rector from school, told us, as you may remember; and this advice is full of sense; I am the proof of it. This morning Mademoiselle Manon told me that Madame Parangon was expected to arrive in two days' time: she had no need to assure me that this news pleased her; her joy appeared on her face and in her eyes. She added, but with an air of confidence and truth that I could not but accept, that she was finally going to be delivered from M. Parangon's persecutions (*persecutions!* that gave me pause); that she would no longer live under the same roof, and that she would no longer be obliged to hide her feelings from someone who merited them. She looked at me as she pronounced these last words, in such a good, sweet, and obliging way that I blushed with pleasure; and Mademoiselle Manon lowered her gaze, blushing as well. Then she continued speaking to me, in these terms: "I will not hide from you, Monsieur" (and this is the first time that she calls me Monsieur), "that it has taken a great deal of strength to resist the attacks of my cousin; (those cursed *attacks* and *persecutions* do not please me); he has sometimes put me in... certain... situations... if we had been surprised, one would have thought... But, thank God, I have extricated myself, by keeping my wits about me, in a way that calms me about things that have always caused me some pain. I would have left the house before my cousin's return; if powerful considerations had not prevented me; I would have had to explain the reasons for my behavior to my mother, to my sister, and perhaps to my cousin herself; and supposing that I had remained silent with them, they would have guessed anyways; for M. Parangon's character is well known; and you understand what that news would have produced in society, and in a household where disunion is ready to break out at any moment; it needs my cousin to hold it together. You will meet her; she is a charming lady, respectable, even though still in the blush of youth; virtuous without affectation, concealing disappointments under an appearance of cheerfulness... which gnaw at her heart; so good is she that one cannot know her without adoring her; so tender, that she seems to be Friendship personified... she is my best friend, I assure you." (O, my Pierre, if this portrait of her is not exaggerated, what joy for me to live in a house governed by so worthy a lady! and then, if she is her best friend, that was not *her* then... you know what I mean?) "M. Parangon does not deserve her" (continued, Mademoiselle Manon). "If you only knew what I know!..." (Here she hid her face in her hands, and I think she sighed); "that Tiennete..." (she picked up again). – "I know, Mademoiselle," (I said), "that he has made propositions to Tiennete..." – "Yes, but what you do not know, Monsieur, is that he seduced that poor girl, and that he took her away from her parents without their knowing it; they are poor people, but they would not have supported such an infamy; he was to receive her on her arrival, and lodged her at the St. Jacques Image, while she pretended not to know him; they passed the night together, with all the necessary precautions in order to save appearances. That girl deceives her corrupter, however; that Loiseau, who follows her everywhere when she goes out, is her favorite." (I was unable to hide my surprise, dear older brother; Tiennete did not tell me her story in this way.) "She has two, and, I believe, dupes them equally." (O, heaven! if that were true!...) "If you doubt what I say for even one moment, it would be easy for me to convince you with your own eyes." – "I accept the proposition, Mademoiselle" (I replied); "for I love to see vice unmasked." – "Believe me, Monsieur" (responded Mademoiselle Manon), "if I did not have good reasons, I would not destroy that poor girl in your mind; I count, what is more, on your absolute discretion; know that today I must go to see my mother, and that they will profit by my absence. Let's come to an understanding; I will ask M. Parangon that you escort me to my home, but you will not leave here. Here is the key to my bedroom; you will enter it without being seen and from there you will see... things that will astonish you, and which made me indignant, on the day that I became a witness by chance, quite in spite of myself..."

Here our conversation was interrupted by the arrival of M. Parangon; and I came immediately here to write you this letter, for fear of forgetting any detail. I will finish it shortly...

I have just returned from having a talk with Tiennete; I spoke at great length with her about Mademoiselle Manon; she responded very little to me; I continued; in the end I think she grew impatient with me, for she said: "My God! I like your way of seeing things! if only everyone had it, we would all be so happy, or tranquil at least: just yesterday, what nice things you said to me about Edmée! Today, it is Mademoiselle Manon; anyone else might think you are fickle; me, I am happy for you, and I say that you see everything in a favorable light." – I felt the reproach, and I was unable to defend myself because I was ashamed; but I acted like city people do, and I hid it under a deliberate attitude. I retorted that Mademoiselle was every bit as charming and gracious as Edmée, if not more; that I did not know this latter person; that it might prove impossible for me to find her again, given all my attempts thus far had failed; and that the former had a character that seemed greater to me with each passing day. Oh! if you could have seen Tiennete turn red, my dear Pierrot! Did she suspect that Mademoiselle Manon knew everything, and that she had told me everything? She blushed, she is guilty; a person does not blush for the things I said, without good reason. I continued to speak about Mademoiselle Manon: Tiennete praised her: she does not like her, but she praises her! My Pierre, it is that she is afraid of her... It is quite magnanimous however to praise those whom one does not like! There are plenty of people who would not do so, no matter what their personal interest. Tiennete did more than that;

she was moved, saying to me: "I would do anything for Mademoiselle; I know her as well as you do; but Madame will return soon... I will always miss Mademoiselle... yes, I love her, and I will prove it." – I don't know what to say. I will put my judgment on hold until I see what I expect. Mademoiselle Manon comes to find me; she is about to depart...

O Pierrot! Pierrot! This is how the world is made!... Eh well, my child, I have seen everything; but absolutely everything one can see. We exited, Mademoiselle Manon and I; M. Parangon went to his friend the doctor's house, a freemason, and one of the best drinkers in town. I quickly returned; I ran to the room; I closed the door with the window, by lock and key, and I drew the curtain. A good hour passed before I heard someone. Finally, Madame Parangon's apartment was opened, and I found myself within range of informing myself. At first I saw M. Parangon; my heart was beating as if it were Mademoiselle Manon or Edmée whom I had seen him with. A hundred thoughts ran through my head, without my settling on a single one of them; for if at one moment I vowed to destroy Loiseau's error, at another moment I resolved to keep silent. Finally, Tiennete appeared; I recognized her by her clothing for her face was covered... I believe, in fact, that she does not agree to such shameless acts with M. Parangon, except against her will; for I saw quite a few struggles, and I even heard what sounded like crying. However, what is the point of prostituting oneself in this way? O Loiseau! poor Loiseau! How she abuses your good faith!... However, there was some funny business involved, which seemed inconceivable to me... I will never again be a witness to such a scene; it made my humanity suffer; I found something revolting in it, on the part of M. Parangon; however I had no choice but to take it all in, for I could not exit from my hiding place; and honestly I would have cursed my curiosity if it had not taught me to know about the people who surround me, and it will prevent me as a result from being the dupe of their grimaces.

At the first opportunity, I ran outside to take some fresh air in the garden of the Cordeliers, our neighbors. I walked around in a sort of daydream: a religious, who goes by the name of Father d'Arras (and who is my confessor) came up to me. He is a man well past middle age, who appears consumed in piety; his conversation is completely edifying; he showed me signs of friendship, made a thousand offers of service, and all that with a politeness that put me at ease with him; one might say that I was obliged to accept them; he asked a lot of questions of me, about our family, our means, my natural talents, and my way of thinking; he appeared very satisfied by the manner in which I responded to him and he made me promise to come and see him often, as a friend rather than as a spiritual Father. His conversation was soothing to my blood, and I found some solace speaking with him.

After taking my leave of him, I returned to Tiennete. Oh! the mask! She had such tranquility, such sangfroid... it is quite unbelievable to behold, how women know how to feign!... Poor Loiseau!... My faith, I don't know what to think anymore of all these magicians (for they are magicians by the spell they cast on their Lovers). If Mademoiselle Manon was false like that!... There is only Edmée who, something tells me, is just as she appears... I am annoyed however to be unable to find her in Vaux; for I feel that it prevents me from abandoning my heart completely to the hopes that Mademoiselle Manon seems to wish to encourage in me, in the event that I should make myself worthy of her love.

And there you have it, my Pierre, news and things of which there is no example back home. I wish you the best, as well as Ursule, and all our brothers and sisters. I need a black suit in addition to the colored one that I received; decency demands that one wear black here on many occasions; as, for example, last week, when the daughter of a sovereign Princess from the Swabian circle in Germany died because of smallpox, at three months old; the Court put on mourning attire for three days; and respectable people, having learned about it on the last day, took three hours to go to the Promenade de l'Arquebuse; and if I had a black suit, I would have escorted Mademoiselle Manon there. I am grateful for the money that you sent me in order to buy buckles; I purchased some very nice ones, and in the latest style; I send back to you those made of copper, which you are kind enough to find good enough to wear yourself. Every time I think of Pierre R***, I tell myself that I have the best of brothers.

XV.

FATHER D'ARRAS TO MADEMOISELLE MANON.

He is a very dangerous friend for Edmond.

I wanted to speak with you yesterday, Mademoiselle, and I was unable to find the opportunity; I have received orders to depart for Saintbris, where I must fill in (despite my repugnance for that office) during a short absence of the curate, and the illness of the vicar. Here is what I wanted to say.

Are you quite sure of your dispositions in favor of the young R***? The secret will remain with me: in a word, this young man, will he be happy? These questions surprise you; but they are founded: on seeing Edmond, I felt that sympathy that an irresistible liking which no one can explain attracted me to him; it is the most tender friendship that inspires me; so I want to serve him by serving you. I know your full worth, my beautiful young lady, and it is a determining motive: but also, Edmond has prejudices: will we succeed in destroying them in time? Time is of the essence. You know how I think: I approve of everything; your reasons will be mine: but watch out! Edmond is not stupid; I have fathomed him. You will say to me – so much the better. Yes, provided that the resolution you have recently given testimony to is as solid, and as durable, as it appeared sincere to me. Do not anticipate regrets for yourself or for me either; I would despair of deceiving Edmond in the sense that I mean; for if he is happy, he will not be deceived.

XVI.

RESPONSE.

O sly serpent!

Your interest in Edmond has gratified me more than you can imagine; he is made to be loved; everyone will have my attention and my heart, when it has to do with that charming young man. Eh! you ask me whether my resolution is firm! Ah! d'Arras, is it really you who asks me this question? It is sacred, this resolution, it is inviolable; believe in its love and honor... which is more dear to me than ever. What the most recent sacrifices have cost me! although they were light in comparison to the others... I deserved this terrible punishment... Edmond will be happy, if my tenderness for him and my faithfulness can help in any way. As for our fortune, which you do not mention, the arrangements would make you ask for moderation... but mama and my sister are absolutely in favor of it. Rest assured; only, heal him of his prejudices, lest there be accidents. I am fiercely afraid of that *virtuoso* Tiennete; girls of that sort, who have made a system of virtue for themselves that suits them, are of unparalleled severity to others. What you know has succeeded; I loathed it; he[14] wanted it; and despite the success, I repent it. Always the... my heart calls them by their right name; you think otherwise, you others; all in good time, if your system is true; But I have difficulty persuading myself of it. Adieu, dear Father: you have so many good qualities, particularly with your friends, for which it is impossible not to forgive you for a number of your faults.

    – Unsigned.[15]

---

[14]Original footnote: M. Parangon

XVII.

Edmond to Pierrot.

*Madame Parangon's arrival. Beginning of a quite
unfortunate passion.*

I am writing to you, my dear older brother, at a moment when the entire house is filled with joy.
Madame Parangon has just returned from Paris. She
is a light brunette, with a perfect face; her eyes possess a gentleness that one could not refuse; her mouth
is slightly large, but attractive; her teeth white, small,
and close-set; her height, taller than average, generous, unapologetic, held better than most women of
that same build. But this portrait is merely a coarse
sketch; one must see her in person, in order to understand what it all adds up to: there is nothing about her
that does not have a particular charm; her fine leg, her
small foot, her bosom, an admirable hand, all these attractions seem to add up in her to a worth that is quite
superior to that of other beauties. What charmed me
most was her smile; it is an enchanting combination
of Ursule's, Mademoiselle Manon's, Edmée's, and
Tiennete's, all of whom have a very pleasing smile.
Add to this that she is in the flower of youth; that she
has a dazzling white complexion, and her skin is of an
incomparably fine and satin texture. She asked to see
us all, one after the other. My comrades and Tiennete
went before me; they each received a present; Tiennete, a beautiful necklace, with stone earrings; l'Al-
garde, the oldest of the Pupils, a handsome snuffbox;
Tintoret, a pretty, fashionable cane. I was envious of

---

[15]Original footnote: Pierre wrote this at the bottom of Letters
whose original was not signed.

the reception she gave them, and I remained completely shamefaced standing behind them. She kissed Tiennete twice, calling her a good friend: I blushed with indignation. But I would be unequal to the task of painting for you a faithful picture of the caresses she gave to her cousin; Mademoiselle Manon seemed a thousand times more lovely in her arms than ever before. Finally, my turn came; I approached her with so timid, so discountenanced an air that she seemed struck. She gave me time to collect myself, saying to her husband: "And this must be the young pupil?" – M. Parangon responded yes, and that he was quite happy with me. Mademoiselle Manon did not fail to reecho these praises, and I am obliged to her for it. "He is my protégé," the lovely Lady resumed, "and I want him to do me the honor." She presented me with a magnificently bound book, telling me that she wanted to encourage the evident predilection that I had for my art, which she had been informed of. She opened it even; and I saw an ample collection of drawings, copies of the masters, such as Raphael, Michelangelo, Correggio, Titian, da Vinci, Buonarotti, Albani, the Carracci, Le Brun, Lesueur, Boucher, Vanloo, etc. I am unable to express to you, my Pierre, just how touched I am by this beautiful gift, and the hand that gave it to me makes it even more precious.

After attending to the people in her household, she appeared at the door; and immediately the room was filled with neighbors. My! how she is loved! My God! what beautiful praise, to loved by everyone! Everyone seemed to see in her a daughter, an adored sister; to young girls, a cherished companion; I was struck with surprise and satisfaction. Finally, everyone withdrew to allow her some quiet time, and I remained alone with her and Tiennete; Mademoiselle Manon having carried to her mother and sister a hundred pretty things that her cousin had destined for them.

At present, my brother, I ask myself how it is that so charming a woman does not command her husband's total affection? It is true that she has been absent for quite a long time; but people say that disappointment had as much to do with it as personal business. Oh! if only he had my eyes!... I feel, while thinking on her, a fire in my bosom, a joy, a pleasure, certain feelings... What a pleasure it is to see her every day, to be able to fulfill several of her commands! The more difficult they are, the more pleasure I find in them. And that makes me understand how our first parents spent their time, pleasantly and without worry, in the earthly paradise; Adam had thoughts for Eve, Eve had thoughts for Adam, just as I have thoughts for her, and they worked, each for the other... But where was I?

Tiennete helped Madame Parangon to get undressed; and I waited there. (I don't know how, honestly, I was capable of that indiscretion!) – "Eh, well, my Tiennete," she said, without appearing to think about me; "You missed me so much! But I'm here now." Tiennete kissed her hand, without saying a word; and I saw tears falling from her eyes. (It is because she feels remorse; she's not yet accustomed to vice, you see: Ah! She must possess quite a bit of it!) "My poor Tiennete," continued my beautiful mistress, "I am insensitive to it at the moment... I would not have believed, however... I am imprudent... I knew him... I should not have... If I am upset, it is not because of that..." Tiennete sighed; she cast a glance at me. Madame Parangon seemed plunged into a deep revery; which she came out of all of a sudden, to address me. She said some very kind things to me, as far as I remember, but I had difficulty hearing her as the sound of her voice brought trouble and emotion to my soul; all the while speaking to me, she was looking for something; she presented to me an incredibly beautiful gold watch, asking me if I was interested in putting it on. And on my response, she fastened it on me; then she entreated me to keep it, adding: "It's on behalf of someone who esteems you that I offer you this present." I responded, "Madame, it will be the most precious thing I possess, as long as I remember that it is from your hand that I received it." With that, I withdrew. I would almost suspect Mademoiselle Manon of having had a hand in this gift, if I wasn't afraid of too much self-pride.

Eh well, what do you say, my Pierre! In all honesty, I do believe that Madame Parangon is the single most completely worthy woman I have met so far. Do you admire that sweetness, that tranquil moderation? She is welcoming to everyone; she caresses Tiennete; she knows everything, but she calls her, "my poor Tiennete!" She blames herself, and says that it is her fault. Eh! the other does not die for shame at her feet! Oh! I would kill myself, I would bury myself one hundred feet underground. Amiable woman, you deserve a crown, a heart... you deserve a man who is worthy of you.

I no longer feel pressed with desire to find Edmée now; and Mademoiselle Manon seems less pretty to me now; the women from our cantons seem less than nothing to me; all the graces gather around Colète C***...

Adieu, dear Pierrot; you were never so tenderly loved by your EDMOND.

XVIII.

PIERROT TO EDMOND.

I continue to submit to error.

I hasten to respond to you, my dear brother; and first of all, I will tell you what I have always told you, that your Tiennete did not deserve what I heard you recount yesterday, and I am delighted that you were not so certain about what you thought you saw Mademoiselle Manon doing; and I would be unable to hide from you that I am surprised to hear you go to such great lengths to praise Madame Parangon, who is a married woman; it is what I would expect from you if she were a girl, or a widow; there is nothing there for you, you do understand me, my Edmond, and I recommend that you don't fill your head with her merits; it is her husband's business to do that; if he does not see it, so much the worse for him. I will also tell you that it seems to me that you are a bit of a weather vane when it comes to friendship; today it is this person, tomorrow that one; and you are wishy-washy in temperament. But I am, however, quite delighted that you are getting along in the city, and I believe even that you will go far; and as you are to live there, it is better that you enjoy it than that you hate it; but do not let the memory of your father's counsels be forgotten, and do not always follow the example of what you see; *be true to yourself*; I have heard it said by old and wise men that we are our own worst enemies; be prudent, and choose someone who will suit you best, either Mademoiselle Manon or Mademoiselle Edmée; you are young, and much too young for marriage, given that you have nothing to speak of in terms of an estate; but, if the opportunity should present itself, and if it should be favorable, it would be more to your advantage in *portraiture* actually than it would set you back, because of the means a woman of leisure gave you. For this reason, focus on behavior, family, possessions; all that is important; and although the last is the least of the three, it is still important. As for myself, I find all that and more in Marie-Jeanne, above all with her kindness, in spite of what you say about the women here; I wish you a woman just like her; or, to bare my heart to you, I wish that Mademoiselle Manon is to your liking; we know her family; she is honorable, and her family has property; [with her] you will go up, instead of down; but keep thinking about it; and when you have decided, you will let me know, and I will speak to our father and mother; and they will send Ursule to be near you. We all embrace you; but, with the exception of Ursule, there is no one among our brothers and sisters who loves you as much as

   – P.R***.

I am delighted to hear about your good reception by

Father d'Arras, and I have reserved this compliment for the end. I have read the part where you speak about him in the your letter, to our good mother; she was filled with joy; she urges you to profit by the counsel of that good Religious, and commends herself to his good prayers.

XIX.

September 29, morning.

Edmond to Pierrot.

He guards himself poorly, and let's himself be seen through.

A weather vane, me, my dear older brother! But, no, I am not at all a weather vane. Must one then close his eyes, and stop himself from thinking? I found Tiennete pretty; Mademoiselle Manon interesting and pretty; Edmée interesting, lovely, and beautiful; Madame Parangon more beautiful, more interesting, lovelier, prettier, and respectable to boot; in a word, a perfect woman. She has perhaps nothing cuter in her traits than what the other three have; for Tiennete is quite cute; Mademoiselle Manon is too; and yet, she has a certain something about her, I don't know what, that speaks to the senses, and which calls out to you, as they say; Edmée has the most beautiful head of brunette hair, coupled with a seductive air of youth and ingenuousness, which is so touching, so touching!... But in Madame Parangon, the attractions are more mature; she has an ease about her and those graces that familiarity with the world gives, especially a sojourn in the Capital, and which no one back home has the slightest idea of, but which makes itself felt, as soon as one sees it; not to mention that her virtue makes an even greater impression on me than her charms. If the beautiful Edmée possessed all that, you would not see me as indecisive as I am... but I have seen her only once, and I am quite content; that said, I will try not to see her again, so as to please you by attaching myself to Mademoiselle Manon, whom I understand you strongly favor. Besides, I feel a pleasure that I cannot explain, thinking that through her I would be Madame Parangon's cousin.

I have no repugnance whatsoever for marriage; on the contrary, despite my youth, it seems to me that I must have that condition to be happy: but, before coming here, I would not have imagined that it would so quickly come into question; how that happens, I do not know. I will tell you that today M. Parangon spoke to me familiarly about his cousin; he clearly explained himself on the subject of marriage, in order to give me to understand that he has his sights on me. Out of fear of making a huge error, however, I responded vaguely; I represented to him that I was still quite young, and without position, and that one is not an artist merely by acquiring the first principles of an art; that I was beginning a long and difficult career, and that it was not certain that I would attain the goal. He told me that he presaged all that I would become one day, and that he was pleased by it. What to say to such consideration, zeal, and good-heartedness? On the one hand, I tell myself that I am not of such salient merit, as they say, to merit that compliment, and that my fortune is not ample enough that one might throw me at a pretty girl without there being some secret reason behind it, which I am unable to fathom; on the other hand, I imagine that I am liked because I strive to be obliging, complaisant, and to apply myself; because I never mock anyone, and I conceal the poor methods of my two comrades: I am flattered that I surpass them (and I believe that I can recognize it myself): Madame Parangon thinks so, as well as Mademoiselle Manon, who comes to dine here every day, ever since she stopped residing here; but this latter person praises me too highly that I could believe her, and I have noticed that Madame Parangon is almost embarrassed by it; she does not encourage it, she who appears so well disposed towards me on all other occasions...

In the evening.

I was interrupted in the middle of my letter; Madame Parangon wanted me to be her rival in the copying of a small painting by Boucher that she wanted to make; I worked the better part of the day, without interruption, but I am not content with myself.

Two times in a row, Mademoiselle Manon had asked me for my arm in order to take a promenade, and I accompanied her with great pleasure. Today, Madame Parangon, before we got up from the table, gave me a pressing commission: I rose immediately, I was so pressed to obey her. On my return, I found her alone; she received me with an open and smiling attitude, telling me that she was not planning to go out, and would I keep her company? Turning red in the face, I stammered something that she did not understand, nor I; I was beside myself, so greatly flattered did I find myself. She sat down, and had me sit down beside her, giving me a book, which she asked me to read. As I was about to begin, Tiennete entered, and she sat down beside her mistress as well, in order to hear me. I could not help reflecting as follows: "How is it that Madame Parangon, so virtuous as she is, knowing this girl, does not send her away? And why does she suffer her to be at her side? It is important to be good; but I do not think that it is good to be weak, or to tolerate vice." The book that was given to me to read has this title: *Lettres du Marquis de Roselle*. I read rapidly. It seemed as though the author had taken all that was said from my heart. But how surprised I was when I saw that that Léonor was nothing but a deceitful person! I glanced at Tiennete on the sly; We were in the middle of the first part; I was asked to stop reading. We spoke about our reading: Madame Parangon expressed the most honest and delicate impressions; to my great astonishment, Tiennete dared to speak in the same way as her mistress; she had the effrontery to go into great detail, which I would have thought more highly of had I not known how things stood. Then, apropos of I do not know what, she spoke about Edmée; she disclosed the background of that lovely girl, and I will convey a part of it to you.

Edmée Servigné is the daughter of a well-off vintner, who can give to each of his two daughters a rather fine marriage. The youngest (the pretty one) received a much better education than her older sister, having been raised by The Ladies of Providence,[16] from six to fifteen years old. It is what makes her live extremely secluded from others and rarely get involved in the games and divertissements of her equals; because, from the moment she socializes with them, she obliges them to distance themselves from the boys they know, whose coarseness is insupportable to her. This young person is well educated, knows a thousand different handicrafts, and would not find herself out of place among honest people (as they say here, when referring to the wealthy); instead, she seems to spend much time with those of her same state: which is perhaps not to her advantage (Tiennete said) and makes her lead a very sad life; she deserves someone who is similar to her.

Indeed, my brother, what a charming girl! and I greatly regret having to renounce her. I want to take some time yet to decide, lest I should prepare myself for a long repentance; and you yourself would not want me to act precipitously.

My respects to our dear father and mother, etc.

XX.

[16]Ladies of Providence: or *Dames de la Providence,* seemingly in reference to the secular house or community, *Maison de la Providence,* founded in 1711, in Lyon, by four pious, high-society ladies with a mission to raise and educate girls (from seven or eight, to twenty-one, years of age) who came from lower-class or artisanal families who were unable to watch over them properly, or who were orphaned, and who were in extreme danger of falling into libertinage or debauchery. -- "Féministes ou notables? Les dames de la Providence à Lyon", by Pioch, Laurence, in *Chrétiens et sociétés*, 11, 2004, 33-48.

THE SAME TO THE SAME.

*What d'Arras was up to. Singular conversation with
a young person.*

I went on a promenade yesterday after supper, for more than two hours, with the good Religious whom I have spoken to you about, my Pierre. I would be hard pressed to relate to you a hundredth of the kindnesses he has shown me; here we are, I think, friends for life, and he has many times assured me of it. He is not one of those scrupulous devotees who forbid every pleasure and who never lighten up; he allows people to relax a bit, and he himself participates in small honest gatherings. For example, after our promenade, we enjoyed ourselves in the convent garden with two or three of his friends, and several Religious whom Father d'Arras had seen passing by, and whom he called out to. He is highly regarded in his house, where the Superiors let him act as he wishes. He comes from a good family, and enjoys a rather important pension, which an only sister, who is very well off, pays him punctiliously. He employs it merely to make friends; also, the best houses in the city open their doors to him; which is no small testimony to his merit. He has told me that he wants to form me, and to procure good acquaintances for me. You see that it is a great boon to me to have pleased him. Madame Parangon, whom he has spoken to about me, does not seem upset that I am in liaison with a man like him, so capable of giving me good counsels.

I am less decided than ever between the little Edmée and Mademoiselle Manon. If the former holds my heart more, the latter is more suited to my advancement in the world. The latter shows me ever more inclination, and she has even rather overtly explained herself to me, by which I can, without presumption, believe that she is thinking of me. I must not hide, and do not wish to hide, anything from you, my friend.

Yesterday, M. Parangon took his wife out for dinner in the city. On leaving, he said to Tiennete that if Mademoiselle Manon should come, she should ask her to remain, and that I would keep her company for dinner. In fact, after I had left Father d'Arras, I found her. She told me, laughing, that she had waited for me with a great deal of impatience, that it was almost seven o'clock, and that she had become apprehensive lest I had done like my two comrades, who were supping away from home. She added that she was going out to take a walk in the garden, while waiting for the time to sit down to table; and she held out her hand that I might accompany her. It began to grow dark. We spoke at first about indifferent things, while walking; after having walked down several alleys, Mademoiselle Manon sat down on a grass terrace; I sat down beside her and we had this conversation: "The Sky is so serene! This autumn is the most beautiful I have ever seen." – "Yes, Mademoiselle, it is the best weather in the world." – "It seems to me that the stars are brighter and more vivid than usual." – "Yes, Mademoiselle." – "'Yes, Mademoiselle!...' but do you know, Monsieur, that you are not responding very well, and that I am looking for a compliment? Is it that you do not know what to do?" – "Forgive me, Mademoiselle: for example, when you spoke to me just now about the beauty of the stars, I was thinking to tell you...” – “To tell me?” – “To tell you...” – “Eh, well? What is it?” – “That the fire in your eyes is brighter and softer than the fire by which they shine.” – “Really, you thought that?” – “Yes, Mademoiselle, but I did not dare to say it.” – “But such things are said, especially in a tête-à-tête; they are said without difficulty... There are other things even, when there are no witnesses, that one can say as well... I would like to be your confidante. Let’s see; let us tell each other all our little secrets: with no reservations; I want to have none with you, on the condition that from your side you hide nothing from me. Have you loved? do you love?... I believe that you are blushing? Come on, no shame; sensibility does no dishonor to a good heart; and then, consider that your sincerity will be the measure of mine.” – “I would love it if...” – “Eh, well, if?” – “If I believed it were reciprocated.” – “I do not believe you are made to be rebuffed.” (Her pretty hand was playing with the rings in my hair, as she said these flattering words.) “She who has touched your heart is not miserable, and if I knew her I would speak to her in your favor.” – “You are very kind, Mademoiselle.” – “But I would wish to be so for her. Are you going to tell me her name?” – “Name her!?” – “Yes.” – “But...” – “You don’t dare?” – “I fear...” – “Fear what? to let her down?” – “There are things...” – “Disabuse yourself; one never let’s a girl down by saying that one loves her, one says it to her face... What is she like?” – “Oh!... charming.” – “Her height?” – “As beauty dictates.” – “I see; she is of advantageous height, without being colossal. Brunette? blonde? Neither the one nor the other perhaps?” – “It is true; her beautiful hair...” (I stopped myself, looking at hers, which is ashen.)... – "Is she rich?" – "More than is needed, for I dare to raise myself to her level." – "You are not ambitious, are you! Have you ever noticed that she took an interest in you?" – "I don't flatter myself." – "But one need not be so modest." – "When one knows oneself, one is always afraid of deceiving himself." – "Must we bring ourselves then to the necessity of bluntly telling you that one loves you? Of repeating it to you, that one loves you? A lover so blockheaded as to bring us to that point, would deserve... on the other hand, presumption is a huge mistake; a presumptuous lover... oh! I would detest him; a lovely reserve has such sweet charms!... provided however that it does not exceed the bounds. For example, I would like a lover (if I had one) to whom I put questions,... with... a sort of stubbornness; as to these questions, goodness... unusual questions, I would like him to understand that I am not guided by a frivolous curiosity... Oh: there's Tiennete coming to announce dinner; after dinner, let us take up our conversation again; and I will make, for my own part, confidences that are bit more clear than yours are."

When we had gone back to the house, I saw the most complete contrast; Mademoiselle Manon was of a joyfulness that made her a thousand times more lovely; Tiennete was of a rather glum sadness that redoubled every time the first one whispered in my ear. This girl ate with us; she left the table early to go to the door where she did not remain for long; she returned with M. Loiseau, whom Mademoiselle Manon received frigidly, although previously she was accustomed to greet him well when he came asking for me. I was surprised that they remained, despite the annoyed attitude that she did not bother hiding from him; when I find myself in these sorts of situation, I am quick on my feet; finally, losing patience, pushed to the extreme, she urged me to give her my hand to escort her home. M. Loiseau was preparing to follow us; she told him, in no uncertain terms, to drop it. He was forbidden it seemed to me. We were about to go; but we noticed that Tiennete had exited: we had to wait for her. On this occasion, I found M. Loiseau quite indiscreet for not withdrawing; he saw our vexation (for I was beginning to show it too) and appeared not to take notice. We were hoping however to convince him to shove off by dint of our severity, when the arrival of Madame Parangon upset our little system completely. She was feeling out of sorts and had left the table [at the restaurant] in order to come home and lie down. She asked M. Loiseau to escort her cousin home; and me, I ran to find some cordials, which she told me she had need of.

Tiennete was standing beside her when I returned; she had no desire to take anything, and appeared quite tranquil to me, so much so that I continued reading in the book that I had begun the night before. On finishing it, I let out, without first reflecting, and completely automatically, "Ah! how happy he is!" They both smiled; and Tiennete said, "Isn't it true, madame, that it that would be a shame!" – "Yes, my friend, I assure you!" responded Madame Parangon. *My friend!* In all honesty, I do not understand that Lady any more than I do Tiennete! Would they happen to be in cahoots, for... No, it is impossible... But softly I hear, in my ears, a certain undertone, that Madame Parangon can no longer stand the caresses of her husband; that she sees, with immense tranquility, another [woman] enjoying her rights; that M. Parangon's disorderliness... I do not know, things that I understand nothing about, have alienated her. But if that were the case, Madame Parangon would no longer be that virtuous female, worthy of so much respect... (my heart rejects the idea, and rises up against it), and Tiennete would be as pitiable as she is culpable. Time will tell.

I confess that after what Madame Parangon and Tiennete said later (for they spoke about Edmée), I find myself less decided than ever. Mademoiselle Manon is really lovely: if you knew how seductive she was, how gracious, when she was chatting with me in the garden! And then, that would make our dear father and mother and you quite happy... I feel however that I would love Edmée better: but that leads nowhere, and when one lives in the city, one must think only of advancing... Oh! if Madame Parangon were only one of them, I know who I would pick!

XXI.

THE SAME TO THE SAME.

He gains control of his heart.

My faith, Pierre, I haven't got any time to breathe, and I am unable to go back on my word, I believe. There is no doubt about it, Mademoiselle Manon is taken with me; M. Parangon, who appeared so cold, so gruff with me, shows an ardent interest in me now:

I am (he says) a presentable partner for his wife's cousin; he proposes to cultivate my predispositions with care, and to reveal all the secrets of his art to me in good time. But in order for you to better understand all that, I will relate to you, word for word, the conversations that I had with the both of them.

As you know, it was Mademoiselle Manon's turn to confide her feelings to me, and you will also remember that we were unable to resume our conversation after dinner. Yesterday, in the afternoon, M. Parangon told me that I was to be ready at seven o' clock because I was going to accompany him to dine in the city. I was surprised, as you may well believe, by so rare a favor; I was all the more so, and quite agreeably, when we found ourselves at the house of Mademoiselle Manon's mother, who greeted me as if I were her son. After the initial polite exchange, M. Parangon passed into the other room with the mother and an older sister; to the effect that Mademoiselle Manon and I were left alone. I had never seen her look so pretty; her toilette had something coquettish and studied about it, which suited her marvelously; I was unable to look at her without admiration; but I kept my silence; she kept quiet as well, and we just looked at each other. For the first time, I saw in her eyes a timid pudor, and on her face a modest embarrassment. In my heart of hearts, I said to her: "Beautiful Manon! ah! how highly now you merit the homage that you no longer appear to demand!" Our silence lasted for a long time. She was the first to break it, and she said to me in an affectionate tone of voice: "You seem to be dreaming, Edmond, am I right? And me, I honestly think that I am sharing in your dream!... You sigh! Would you care to tell me what the happy object of that sigh is!... You don't say a thing!" – "Apparently, Mademoiselle, one finds difficulty expressing himself when he has too many feelings." – "Feelings! It is quite sweet, Edmond, to have tender feelings; sweeter still to bring them out into the open; delicious for lovers to savor them together..." – "Let's talk then." – "What have you got to tell me?" – "But, if I dare say so, it is I who ought to be asking you that question." – "'If I dare'! You're too distant, Edmond." – (I drew near to her; she smiled as if that was not what she had meant.) – "Eh! why then would you hesitate to ask me some questions?" – "Well, given that you embolden me... I believe it is you who owe me a confidence." – "So you remember!... are you still thinking about that madness?" – "Wisdom or madness, it interests me." – "Ah! how I adore it when you act like that!... Eh, well, hold it right there, that's how I would desire you..." – "If I had the good fortune, would you satisfy my ardent curiosity, Mademoiselle?" – "If you really pressed me, I could become indiscreet." (I kissed her hand.) "Is this how you press me? More self-restraint." (I turned red in the face, and I was afraid I had offended her.) She resumed: "I see clearly that one must give in... however, it is proper that things should be equal between us; you will ask me questions, as I did of you, and you will guess at a half-word: Come on, let's begin." – "Mademoiselle, what is your secret?" – "Edmond!" – "Yes, what is its nature?" – "But, must I answer that?" – "Yes, and sincerely." – "Well, I think that it has to do with... loving." – "You think? You're not sure?" – "I suppose that I am." – "You love?" – "I love." – "Much?" – "Much." – "A man?" – "A young man." – "How fortunate he must be!" – "That is no longer a question, and I do not know how to respond." – (I kept quiet for several minutes; then I replied:) "Does he know how fortunate he is?" – "He should." – "You have deigned to inform him, no doubt?" – "Yes, but only recently." – "How did he receive this precious assurance?" – (She remained quiet for a moment before responding:) "He alone could tell." – "You doubt that he loves you! Ah! You who are made to make everything submit to your charms!" – "Since I know him, I begin to distrust their power." – "Would you be constant?" – "Unto the grave." – "In what way do you love him?" – "For himself." – "Is he the first to reign over your heart?" – "But, what sort of questions are these... Eh, well, yes; what he inspires in me, I have never felt it before." – "Is he young?" – "My same age." – "His face?" – "Too good." – "His attitude?" – "Quite fine, and it will become charming." – "His mind?" – "He has one; but its brilliance is yet to be seen." – "... I cannot guess." – "You give up so quickly!" – "Where can this so-perfect lover be found?" – "Perfect! I did not say that; but he is on his way to becoming it." – "Eh, well, this lover then, is he worthy?..." – "Yes, Monsieur, he merits the feelings that he inspires in me; he is deserving... I regret all the moments in my life when I did not know him." – "Ah! Mademoiselle! you make me jealous of your happiness." – "You poor blind man! How can that be?" – "Where is he now, who has such a glorious fate!" – "Sitting beside me."

My dear Pierrot, my eyes clouded over, and the objects around me became blurry. I felt Manon's hand in my fingers and my lips pressed it; I fell to her knees, struck, and was beside myself. My charming mistress leaned over; her pretty mouth approached my cheek, saying to me, – "Get up, my friend; yes, it is you whom I love; it is you about whom, at this moment, M. Parangon sounds my mother's dispositions, in order to bring her to accept you as a son-in-law." – "What happiness!" I cried out. "Ah! From now on, my only preoccupation will be you! What joy for my parents, how happy my mother will be, to have you as a daughter!" – And as I was about to show her the letter you had sent me, in which... it was that then her mother, her sister, and M. Parangon came back into the room. All three had a slightly pensive look; nevertheless, the two Ladies bestowed a thousand caresses on me, above all the mother. During the meal, Mademoiselle Manon was blushing profusely, and she almost did not open her mouth; if she dared to look at me once, it was on the sly. When we had quit the table, it was nearly ten o'clock; M. Parangon and I prepared to leave; but as we were on the point of exiting, Madame Palestine removed from an armoire several very beautiful cuffs, embroidered by Mademoiselle Manon herself, which she gave to me as a present: it is an admirable handiwork; I did not know how to thank her.

On our return, M. Parangon asked me what I thought of the people whom we had just supped with. I responded that they were very fine Ladies; that Madame Palestine was a respectable woman who reminded me of my mother; that Mademoiselle Manon was a young lady, like my sister Ursule; and that Mademoiselle Claudon, her older sister, appeared to me to be of good character, with a very sweet disposition. – "Eh, well," he continued, "they like you too: I consider your parents, and I want to treat you as if you were my son; I have resolved to give you to Manon. After your wedding, you will reside at your mother-in-law's place; you will live there as if at your father and mother's, in a word, as a son and brother; I will redouble my efforts to form you; you will be able to dedicate yourself to the study of our art without another care in the world, by means of the ease that this marriage will give you; for Madame Palestine, who already regards you as a support to her in her old age, will arrange things quite nicely for you; she is rich, and her oldest daughter, who is of failing health, is planning for a life of celibacy; you will inherit everything one day. Without such great advantages, however much goodwill I feel for you, I would not press: but one must seize the bull by the horns when the opportunity presents itself; unless... you're against the idea." – I thanked M. Parangon for his good offices; I said that Madame Palestine and Mademoiselle her sister did me much honor, and that I would strive to be worthy of their esteem. "If that is how it is, I will tell you everything," M. Parangon replied; "my wife, to whom I communicated my plans, made several objections... Women are like that, my boy; they accept you, they smile at you; you believe that they are well disposed in your favor, and suddenly you realize that you have nothing in your hands. For example, is it not true that you thought my wife would desire what was best for you? And yet she is opposed to it: even the good Tiennete, in front of whom I spoke, gave her opinion: 'Our cousin could easily find an important match: a Lawyer, a Doctor, who knows?'" – "That does not surprise me, Monsieur," I said; "your kindnesses for me are so great..." – "Let's leave my kindness out of it: for I must tell you plainly, Manon loves you, and I am merely satisfying her desires, which she has fought against for a long time now; that poor Child was afraid of me. The innocent girl hardly knows me! I have a long vision; you are a good subject; if you work hard, one day you will surpass such as believe themselves to be so much better than you: look at the Vanloos, the Bouchers, the Vernets and many other artists in Paris, how they are sought out by the Greats... I am giving you a charming woman, who loves you; I give her a husband who cannot help loving her, and who will make a way for himself in the world. Look, my boy, one must love the person one marries; Madame Parangon did not love me; I loved her, I did, with the best faith in the world: in the end, I realized that I was the only one in love; my faith, I became cold, like marble, and I grew unhappy in that situation; I grew unhappy, nobody could say just how much... I raised that little Manon; I watched her grow from an early age; I attached myself to her like a father to his daughter, and I think that I make her happiness by giving her to you. Is it not the case that my wife has become jealous of her sometimes? But jealous, to the degree that she imagines things... She finds falsity at every turn; but, fundamentally, I fear that she does not love her." – "I believe, Monsieur, that you do not do your wife justice: I saw the welcome she gave to Mademoiselle Manon, and..." – "You poor credulous thing! As I said! Women! They administer caresses so as to better tear each other apart; they embrace, but would prefer to strangle one another. But enough of this talk; keep it a secret until we are sure: for our business is with women whose mind, a real weathervane, turns whichever way the wind blows. If they were to go back on their word, they would be unable to boast about having refused us; in particular my wife, and her worthy confidante, – mum is the word. I will let your parents know; you would do well to write to them too."

We found ourselves at that moment before the door to the house. Madame Parangon and Tiennete were inside reading, waiting for us. Without her questioning us, M. Parangon lied to his wife. My Pierre, although I now know that she is not as keen about me as I had originally thought, I could not help wondering: "How can someone lie to so lovable a wife! I never want to keep any secrets from mine."

Yes, now you see me quite decided; Mademoiselle Manon is what I need. Mention it to our dear father and mother, and make them understand that there is no longer anything that should stand in the way of their sending Ursule to the city. Mademoiselle Manon will acquaint her in no time with the customs and habits here; they will become fast friends, and our union will be happier because of it. We can be married, you and I, at about the same time, my dear older brother. I embrace you very tenderly.

P.S. Father d'Arras introduced me to a very interesting man newly arrived in Paris, who goes by the name of M. Gaudet: he is an engraver, very skilled in the art, even though rather young, and extremely rich: he has accepted me as a friend, on the recommendation of the Father who begins, as you see, to act on the promise he made me.

XXII.

Pierrot to Edmond.

Through ignorance, I assist in pushing him over the edge.

I make you this quick response, my poor Edmond, to tell you that I see you now at the point where I wished you to be. May the Lord bless our marriages, the both of us, and may our betrotheds be under His holy protection. And as for the good Father Religious, our good mother and I, we are very pleased with the friendship that you have made with him, and he with you; and we believe that he will attract God's blessings to you; and that is already a very good start. As for the dear Demoiselle Manon, it seems to me that she must efface all thought of others from your mind; after reading your two last letters, I would have almost wished that Marie-Jeanne were a little more like her: but that's not the fashion that girls here say such charming things to boys, and then this, and then that, so graciously that my ear feels like it has been tickled. We received a few lines from M. Parangon, in which he states what he has done for you; and our father, after having read them to our mother, made us all gather round to hear him read it aloud; and he told me after supper to read in the Bible the chapter about the marriage of Isaac with Rebecca; and while I was reading, we saw him wipe away the tears. And then we said a prayer as usual, and at the end of it, he gave us all his benediction, and turning toward Ursule, whom he wants to send to you in the coming days, he asked her again to bring to you what he has given you a second time. We were all touched, and we wept for joy; and then we all embraced, and then one after the other we embraced our father and our good mother. They will not depart for another one or two weeks, to meet the request, because of our grape harvests. You will need to come and meet Ursule, whom I will escort tomorrow afternoon as far as Saintbris. I will tell you the rest in person. We all love you with all our heart; love us as well, and above all,

– Your brother PIERROT.

XXIII.

October 10.

M. GAUDET TO MADEMOISELLE MANON.

Edmond's true corrupter appears.

You admit it, charming cousin, that you have need of my assistance? What would d'Arras have done? Men of the robe always have scruples. I will not fail to show up on your important day; but there is no need for me to appear beforehand, on account of the beautiful Parangon. The young man is her protégé, she knows everything; she would shed light on all our plans from up close. I am quite pleased with your suitor; he has character; but he also seems to me like those knaves who must keep nothing but the wings of their love. Trust me, you could deceive him a little, doing without all those little scruples that you have shown me; he will not be in arrears for long. As for the prejudice under discussion, I have already begun to address it; but these people from the countryside hold on to it with a tenacity! Except for that, I would say to you, follow your heart rather than prudence. I am quite surprised that after having shown that young famished fellow a honeycomb, he has not acted like a Jonathan:[17] apparently the French are not as gourmand as the Jews. That there, however, was the most sure tranquilizer. If we could make him spend several months in the Capital, you could profit thereby by spending your crucial moment in retreat; but you find his staying there too dangerous for faithfulness.

Papa Parangon has taken the wise course of action, and his trip is well thought out. Time is of the essence, you navigate between Charybdis and Scylla.

P.S. I hear d'Arras was kind enough to mention my name to your betrothed: encourage in him an absolute silence to the latter about your affairs; let me reveal our kinship to him, when the time is right; I will do it in such a way as not to ruin anything.

XXIV.

The following day, 10 o'clock in the morning.

EDMOND TO PIERROT.

Fine beginnings on the one hand; behind-the-scene

---

[17]Jonathan: 1 Samuel 14:25.

maneuverings on the other.

Ursule has arrived here, my friend, at ten o'clock in the morning. From the pleasure that I felt embracing her, the only thing missing was your presence. Why then was it not you who accompanied her? I was expecting to see you at Saintbris, and I was ready to leave when Ursule and our younger brother Bertrand entered M. Parangon's house: I will even acknowledge that I was quite surprised that our wise parents had let Ursule and Bertrand set out on their own: what would these two children have done if bad sorts had attacked them in the wood of the Fée,[18] in the thick of that valley where men never pass without some terror?[19] But they arrived safe and sound, thank God. Madame Parangon was alone in the salon; it was she who received them. Our Ursule approached her blushing; she asked for her brother, without naming me. The lovely Lady to whom she addressed herself did not wish to draw out her embarrassment; certain traits that we share, and which she had noticed in my sister, made her immediately put two and two together; she asked Tiennete to fetch me. When I appeared, I found her seated beside my good mistress, who was telling her very flattering things. Ursule got up quickly from her seat; she threw herself around my neck and kissed me twice, before I could get let out a word. – "It is quite clear," said Madame Parangon, smiling, "that Mademoiselle does not like her brother at all." –

---

[18]Original footnote: Or *Fáe*, as some people pronounce it by corruption.

[19]Original footnote: Many murders had taken place there, one as recently as 1772.

"Ah!, Madame," replied the innocent girl, very seriously, "after my father and mother, there is no one in the world more precious to me." – "You are tired, my lovely girl," responded Madame Parangon, "come upstairs with us." And seeing that Ursule was watching whether I would follow them or not, Madame Parangon said, "You must separate from your dear brother for just an instant: we will not hesitate to call him."

So flattering a welcome for one of my own kin filled me with more happiness than all the kindnesses that Madame Parangon had shown me to date. At the end of half an hour, Tiennete came down to tell me that I could go up. Madame Parangon left us alone in the room, saying that we needed to catch up in private. In fact, my sister was to confide in me something that I was not expecting. After having assured me of the warm feelings of our respectable father and good mother, that of her own, and that of our brothers and sisters, Ursule related to me the conversation she had just had with Madame Parangon, and this is what she said: "After we came up here, Madame renewed her caresses, and confessed to me that I had given her an immense pleasure coming straight to her house. 'I consider you,' she added, 'a gift from Heaven; it is I who wants to serve you here like a mother and sister. Reciprocate the feelings that you begin to inspire in me, and this day will be one of the happiest days of my life. I have a sensitive heart; to love, for me, is a necessity; but one half of the human race is forbidden to me, because I am married, and my sex hadn't yet accorded to me but this one girl... Tiennete,' she said, interrupting her discourse; 'sit down beside us... You see this girl: she is not at all what she seems; I esteem her; she is my companion, my consolation, my only friend; make her your friend too; she merits it. But I must tell you that we will lose her very soon. I alone would have missed her; we will miss her together. My soul wishes to be united only with pure souls like your own, adorable girls... My beautiful Ursule, you will not go and stay at the house of those whom it was proposed that you live with... no, you will not go... you must promise me. Leave the determination of your fate to me; let the most tender friendship arrange it... You are surprised, of course, by the warmth I show you, before I even know you; I do not stop and ask myself for the reason even; it is enough for me that I feel it, that I love you, and that I will consider you as the equal of my younger sister Fanchette, whom I love most dearly. You may count on the steadfastness of my dispositions toward you... At present, it is your turn to speak; I wait for you to explain to me your feelings...' – 'I am confused, Madame, by such a show of kindness,' I responded to her; 'with all my heart I wish to acknowledge it, and my entire ambition is to be worthy of it; to obey you will be my law.'"

"I do not know," my sister continued to tell me, "what was so delightful to that Lady about so simple a response from me; but she looked at Tiennete and exclaimed, 'Her personality is just like her appearance!' Then she embraced me and immediately you were called up..."

I remained speechless by Ursule's discourse, dear older brother. It plunged me into a chaos of emotions, which I cannot disentangle: that Tiennete should be estimable! That she should be the friend and the consolation of her mistress! I see that Madame Parangon is clearly the dupe of that girl: she is ignorant of her husband's new distractions; she speaks only of his past ones, if one connects the dots, which I had so clearly noticed from the start. Virtue, then, will always be the dupe of hypocrisy! That my sister should be Madame Parangon's friend, that is a happiness that enchants me; she could never find a more virtuous woman, nor a more respectable protectress; but for her to be the friend of Tiennete!... Oh! What an abyss the feminine heart is! But consider, I pray you, how an unfortunate penchant is enough to degrade us? Without Tiennete's foibles, Ursule should be honored to be her friend; without M. Parangon's excessive desire, not for love, but for women, he would have none of the fundamental shortcomings that he does; but it is this ill-controlled and displaced desire of his that engages him in card games, which M. Gaudet assures me that he does not care for, and in an excessive consumption of wine, which leads him to gambling, which bores him; it is the same, but depraved desire, that makes him insensitive to the attractions of his incomparable spouse... Yes, my brother, as entirely taken as I am with Mademoiselle Manon, if her cousin were a maiden, and I should dare to presume... but you have forbidden me from entertaining such ideas as these. I will continue with what she said to my sister.

It is with the greatest astonishment that I hear this, that Madame Parangon does not want Ursule to live with my betrothed. (It is true that she does not know on what terms I now stand with Mademoiselle Manon.) Nevertheless, I would like to let her be mistress; and I entreat our father and mother to oppose nothing that she will appear to desire. To disoblige Madame Parangon! I believe that I would prefer to die... so good a heart! so beautiful a soul!... I said as much to our sister...

[As Madame Parangon absolutely does not want Bertrand to return home today, despite the representations I made to her, that he had a carriage... I will be unable to finish my letter until this evening.]

At ten o'clock in the evening.

Women are really quite singular! show them some deference, submission, or simple trust, and they abuse it! This morning, M. Parangon had departed for the countryside before my sister arrived (I had forgotten to mention this); consequently, he did not meet her. Having gone back downstairs again at around eleven o'clock, and after having written to you, I found Madame Parangon alone in the salon. – "We have upstairs," she said to me, "the prettiest villager in all the world; when she first made her appearance, I thought I saw the perfect image of one of the nymphs of Mythology: the harmonious sound of her voice, her modestly lowered eyes, her embarrassment, the candors that sparkled in all that she says and does, struck me as never before. The two chats we have had together attach me to her forever. Tiennete currently sees to her toilette; you will see her; the lovely Ursule's clothing are simple and unremarkable; but how she embellishes them!" – I could not help from responding: "Madame, these last words of yours are also what were said about you to Tiennete one day." – "You address my compliments for Ursule to me... There is something I wanted to ask of you: nobody knows that your sister is here, correct?" – "That is correct, Madame." – "Will you grant me my wish?" – "Me, Madame! You have the kindness to forget that your wish is my command." – "Edmond, you were raised in a village, and I want to believe that that is not one of those phrases that merely sounds good, but means nothing, as it does in the city; so I take what you just said as meaningful, and I thank you." – "Madame," I returned, "deign always to remember, that executing your orders is for me..." – "You must not," she interrupted me, "let M. Parangon know that your sister is here, nor that he see her; nobody must know about it besides us, that is, you, Tiennete, and me; absolutely nobody. I command that of you." (I was completely forbidden, and I said nothing in reply; she continued). "From tomorrow on, she will go to live with an aunt of mine whom I dearly love; she will be a new friend for Ursule, whom I will never be jealous of; but I will be just the opposite; do you understand me? Let your parents know: Ursule is mine; she has consented to be so; she is mine alone, and yours, of course; she will dine upstairs with your younger brother, and you here with me; we will spend the afternoon with her; but I want to keep her from the eyes of everyone in the house. Go and see her for a moment, and then come back downstairs to table."

How surprising and strange, my dear older brother! Me, who was counting on my sister going to strengthen my marriage with Mademoiselle Manon, by gaining her friendship and that of her mother... It does not make any sense! So, I will be married, I will see my sister, and I will be able to hide her from my wife! In order to do that, we would need to live in a city as immense as Paris. And why all the mystery? In truth, every woman is a woman, and Madame Parangon is like any other... My fingers shake as I write these last words; it seems like I am blaspheming a more-than-human being. Indeed, what she has said to Ursule, the empire she has already taken over her person, all that confounds me, surprises me, and forbids any murmur from me. On drawing close to Ursule, I found that she had red eyes, as if she had been crying; however she appeared extremely joyous to me. She said to me, taking me by the hand: "My Brother, on coming here, I could not contain the joy that I felt with each step I took, approaching you: I did not suspect, however, another happiness that was waiting for me, and that you prepared for me without knowing it. My friend, you have opened two hearts to me that are not difficult to know... in one single moment, my own has found unison..." (She stopped for a moment, looking at me; then she resumed). "Edmond, everything that Madame has just told you, is reasonable; we must not hesitate; for I will tell you that we are fortunate, the both of us, to have found so virtuous a friend... Without her, the city,... based on what people say,... men... women... all that makes me shudder." And looking at my younger brother, she said, "Go, my dear Bertrand, return to the village, and do not be tempted to leave it; you would not have the same fortune as our Edmond: I would follow you, I would abandon all the hopes that I have been made to conceive, if I had not found a good guide, whose only desire is Edmond and my advantage: the Lady of this place is a protectress over me, whom I love already like a mother." – "It is a spell," I let out involuntarily! My sister and brother, they both had the same eyes, the same heart!... Tiennete was standing behind me; she served the table and sat down with Ursule and our brother Bertrand, while reminding me that dinner was being served downstairs. I descended.

As soon as my colleagues had taken up their work again, Madame Parangon led me to my sister. We were together for hardly one moment when Tiennete appeared to tell me that Mademoiselle Manon had just arrived. Madame Parangon seemed troubled; Ursule blushed; they glanced at each other. After a moment of indecision, the former told me to go and entertain her cousin, to engage her to take a walk in the garden, under the pretext of the beautiful weather we were enjoying, while she, my sister, and Bertrand would exit and go to Madame Canon's place (that's the name of the aunt that she had spoken to me about), where I would go to join them later, when I was free. I flew to be beside my dearly betrothed. You have no idea of the pain that I felt being obliged to use disguisement with her, and to hide my sister's arrival from her; especially at certain moments when she showed me so much affection, trust, attachment, as never before... Oh! I love her now for life, my Pierre. She thought I was alone, and was the first to propose our taking a walk in the garden. We sat down under a trellis where the most beautiful muscat grapes hung. During our chat, Manon looked at them with a face of desire. She let go of my hand; she responded to me in broken phrases only. "What is it?" I said to her, smiling. – "Don't you see that I desire them?" – "And what is it that you desire?" – "You cannot guess." – She cast a quick glance at the grapes, and immediately lowering her eyes, I saw them moist with tears. I got up on the jiffy and picked the most beautiful grapes I could find, which I set on her apron. She could not hide a look of satisfaction; with each grape that I gave her, "More," she said to me, "I want more." – She ate, or rather devoured, two of them; but she wanted me to receive from her hand each seed from the third. As for the rest, she could not be bothered, and she beseeched me to remove them from her sight. I discovered quite a little unusualness in all this; but I found an immense pleasure playing along. Then we chatted, as you will hear.

"My cousin[, M. Parangon,] is in the country-side," she said to me. – "Yes, he departed this morn-ing." – "Does anyone know where he went?" – "I have no idea, Mademoiselle: but Madame..." – She vigorously interrupted me: "Madame does not know either." – "What business is that of ours, his trip," I said, laughing. "Other than you, what must I busy myself with?" – "I like what you say there, Edmond; but on speaking about my cousin's trip, I am speaking about things that concern you. It is to visit your par-ents that M. Parangon went. We will be happy; I be-gin to believe it: I had not yet dared to abandon my-self to this hope; but the secret that you have kept, as-sures us of our plans. Do not trust my cousin, Madame Parangon: she is unusual, capricious; she has but this one fault: she would be perfect if not for that:

M. Parangon and I, we would really like it, if at all possible, that she does not know about our marriage except on the day itself." – "Your wish is my command," I replied, "but why hide it from her? I know that she loves you." – "I believe so, too, but... she sometimes has strange ideas... Must I say it? I have committed several wrongs against her, and I confess it to my friend... Ah! if only I had known you sooner!... I sincerely love you; let the secret of our hearts be between you and me only; if it was known to a third, whoever it might be... you do understand me, whoever it might be... you would lose me... In several days, we will be completely one, each one for the other; and you will feel that from that point of view, there is no one in the world whom your interests affect as much as me. So believe in a pure, in a heroic love; but do not believe in a disinterested friendship." – "As I adore you, my beautiful mistress, whence comes all this talk, which troubles my mind?" – "Let this kiss dispel it. Edmond! ah! if your heart were like mine, one word could assure us forever of our mutual esteem... But you have not lived enough. One will never be able to find in the same object, then, your innocent candor, the absence of prejudices... which are based on, I want to believe;... but based on... based on chimeras, after all, when... Hapless me!" – "You! Hapless! You who make me so happy, you would never be hapless, dear Manon!..." – "I must confess to you, Monsieur, that you are not the first person who has moved this heart which adores you, you and you alone, today..." – "But you love me?" – "More than my life." – "Previously, before leaving my home in the country, this avowal would have pained me; but today, since you love me, and me alone, that's all that I could ask for." – "What a happy augur! You would not be jealous then, of this... [other] attachment (very different from what I have for you)..." – "Since you first loved me?" – "I would be unworthy." – "No, given that you love me, and me alone, today, I am the happiest of men." – "Eh, well, my dear lover, no more secrets from you... I want to unburthen my heart to you: you should know then that... but first, you will receive an oath that I will never break,... will you still love me?" – "I swear to you in turn," I replied, "by what is most sacred." – "It's done then," and she resumed...

I could not believe my eyes, my dear brother: Manon, the proud Manon, appeared to want to get down on her knees! I saw this movement like a flash of lightning; I held her in my arms; I set her on the bench; and I took up a position more fitting for myself, not her. She wrapped her arms around my neck: "You love me," she said to me, "never stop telling me so: by dint of hearing it, I will persuade myself perhaps... my spouse... my friend... a tender, indulgent friend: forgive me an error... which I abhor."

We were at this point when we heard someone walking by the gate. I got up; I saw Father d'Arras, who was approaching the trellis. He had come from Saintbris expressly to see us. Manon and me, we went forward to meet him. He appeared delighted to find us together. It appears that M. Parangon, in passing, had communicated to him our marriage, under the seal of secrecy; for he gave us some very good instructions about the duties of spouses. The manner in which we listened to him appeared to him a good sign; he slipped in several very delicate praises to Mademoiselle Manon; she, while blushing, but with a certain grace however, and in order to hide from me her trouble, she begged me to go and cull for her the most beautiful flower of the season, which was growing at some distance from us. I do not know what she asked of the good Father; but as I was returning, I heard him respond to her: "Absolutely not." It would seem to be some cases of conscience that he was deciding on. Manon left me almost immediately after that; the good Religious went to vespers, and I ran to Madame Parangon's aunt's house.

I found my sister and her new protectress alone, on the one side; Bertrand with the good Lady Canon on the other, chatting peacefully. I was told that I had made them wait for a long time. I responded that Father d'Arras had come to join us in the garden. This response appeared to satisfy. – "Well, my dear Edmond," said the good Lady Canon to me, "how goes it?" – "Slowly, Madame." – "Not in all cases, my child: but beware a pot of pitch! Not everyone sees eye to eye. When the cat is away, the mice will play. The sparrow makes its nest in that of the swallows. The cuckoo hatches its eggs in the greenfinch's. He who flatters us wants to deceive us. Mistrust is the mother of surety. Do you understand me?" – "Perfectly well, Madame; everything you say there is quite true; for those are proverbs." – "Listen to my niece, she is a good woman; do you understand me? Listen to her... My faith, yes! At eighteen years old, a boy like you, about to tie the knot! How nice to see children marry! But come on, a wife is a deceptive piece of merchandise: whoever does not have one, itches for one; and whoever has one repents of it. I have been a wife (for one is no longer a wife at my age), and I know them well; they will *dupe* you, poor Men! Hmm! The serpents! Listen, I knew one, and I know one still..." – Fortunately, Madame Parangon and my sister interrupted her by approaching, if not for which I would have had to endure another deluge of proverbs. It appears that the secret of my marriage had gotten out, that it had been discussed since Ursule's arrival, and that it is disapproved of. What consoles me is that our sister does not know that it is about to take place so soon. However, I feel a very keen pain; it is that Madame Parangon sees that I hide things from her. This thought torments me. Nevertheless, I will wait for M. Parangon's return, before hazarding anything.

So this is my news, my dear Pierrot; and we are not at the end of it. I predict some difficulties; but I am quite determined.

P.S. Ursule is staying at Madame Canon's now, where Madame Parangon wants her to reside.

XXV.

Pierrot to Edmond.

M. Parangon's finesse.

As I can see by your letters that we are no longer employing our ordinary preambles. So as I write these lines to you, and others, I will omit them from mine.

I had just returned home, my dear Edmond, after having conducted Ursule and Bertrand to the top of the hill, when we saw your Master arriving, the good M. Parangon, who came in person to encourage our father and mother to depart with him the day after tomorrow, with the purpose of concluding your alliance with Mademoiselle Manon; you will have one bann on Sunday, and dispense with the two others, in order to be married one week from Tuesday. And that is why, my dear brother, unbeknownst to them, I send this letter to you by Georget, so that you might surprise him, by going out to meet them at the edge of the woods. Our father will be on horseback, and our mother will be riding her usual mount; for the horses that carried Ursule in the covered carriage were too tired to go, arriving only this evening; to the effect that our mother could be made uncomfortable for four leagues, where there is no village, if I had not provided for her; I will tell you then, that I had an arbor of hazel and young hornbeam constructed, with branches of fruit-garnished vine, which I cut; and this arbor is located at the inside corner of the Provenchère woods, right where I brought you, when you were going to reside in the city; for since then, that place has always held a kind of tender memory for me which gives me both pain and pleasure at the same time. To-morrow, towards morning, I will have had brought a nice little breakfast there; and those who will have brought it will have left by the time you arrive, by another road; and you, you will stand at the entrance of the arbor; and when our father, our mother, and M. Parangon approach, you will play on your flute that tune that mother likes so much. They will be quite surprised; I will pretend to be surprised like the others; and when they see all that, they will have a good deal of satisfaction, and they will partake of an agreeable repast in that poor countryside. My dear brother, I have but one regret, it is to be unable to be present at your marriage. I must manage the house in our father's absence, and watch over the new wine, and make progress in the sowing of uncultivated fields; we are at the busiest time of the year now, as you well know; so if we let one good day go by, I am not sure how to make up for it. But standing in for me, I have obtained from Marie-Jeanne that she would be at your nuptials; and her father and mother are all for it, because I am not going, and nobody will have anything negative to say about it in the village on her account. There also you will have all our brothers and sisters ready to go; except for Christine and Marianne, they will not depart until two days before your beautiful day: our father has designated our brothers Georget and Bertrand; not to mention our sisters Christine and Marianne, Brigite, Marthon and Claudine; the only ones to remain with me at home will be Augustin-Nicolas, and the little Charlot, with Babette and the little Cathiche, – who are quite upset about it; they go and caress mother, they cry, they employ all their little tricks; they have even gone to entreat M. Parangon, who really wanted to intercede on their behalf. But our father, a bit severe in this respect, as you can well imagine, made all that fuss stop immediately. We are all going to accompany our father and mother for part of the journey, to that point where the arbor is, with the exception of Georget, who has offered to manage the house in my stead. If I do say so myself, my Edmond, despite their jerkins and village costumes, I do not believe that anyone will find Marie-Jeanne and our sisters badly off in the city; M. Parangon cannot stop admiring them; he says also that he is dying to meet Ursule. I wish you, my friend, the fulfillment of all your desires, and I embrace your dear betrothed; while urging you to take good care of Marie-Jeanne, and also Ursule; for you know how timid she is. If Mademoiselle Manon were to be found there under the arbor with you, our joy would be complete tomorrow; but I don't recommend it.

XXVI.

The same day as the previous.

M. PARANGON TO MLLE. MANON.

Here is what they were planning for my brother.

My trip was most successful, and these good folk here do everything one could wish for, when they believe it to be in their children's best interest. Eh, well, you sulky young lady, have I kept my word? It is true, and I admit it, that I am merely fulfilling a duty; but after all, the manner and ardor that I put into it, does it not deserve some gratitude? I would not employ this word, which seems to carry the idea of a reproach, if I did not perceive for some time now a rather cold reserve by you with respect to myself. I cannot believe that as hardened a young lady as my pretty cousin is, you would let your heart be taken by the starling whom we so well lime. In any case, one thing must not get in the way of the other; you understand me in any case. One piece of advice that I give to you, and which is not to be neglected, is to come before the good folk; there is no doubt about the suitability, they will be overjoyed; we will take possession of them, so that they see at the right time and place the proud Juno: your seductive appearance will lure them into our nets, not to mention your precious way of speaking and your little prudish attitude, which makes you desirable in the eyes of high-society people, but which will subjugate people from the country even more so. I have put some order into what you know, so as to hasten the celebration: but the Devil is quite cunning and Women even more (said with no intention of offending you), and you know this from experience; your charming little tricks surpass the finest so well recounted by Boccaccio and Lafontaine. Here then is what I believe it is appropriate for you to do. Your mother is always furious, am I right? My faith! So much the worse for her! But she is a good woman; she makes a stifled sound and swallows her tears in front of everyone. Adieu, my little chicken: but a little more openness with me: a handsome little urchin is not up to the task of chasing me from your heart.

P.S. His sister Ursule is in the city now; you will have seen her doubtless: that little Bear's face is praised to high heaven here. (Forgive me the poor witticism on her name, which means precisely that.) She is said to be the prettiest among the girls here, who are all quite fine looking.

XXVII.

Pierrot to Edmond.

His change [in attitude] begins to strike me.

There was no opportunity for me to say one word to you at our encounter; and as a result I am going to make up for it with this letter. And to start, I begin by confessing my surprise (quite agreeable) of having found Mademoiselle Manon under the arbor, together with Madame her mother and Mademoiselle her sister: but what I do not understand is how those Ladies could not have met our Ursule! When they said as much, I had not yet opened your letter, which I did not receive until then; and since having read it, I am no less surprised, but in another way. What does it mean, and what is it exactly that Madame Parangon is conspiring to do? And you, you yield like that, to a woman who means nothing to you? Would it not have been more appropriate for Ursule to have accompanied those Ladies when they came to meet our father and mother? Your judgment was sorely lacking there, my Edmond. And then I found you with a disdainful and nonchalant attitude; it was your betrothed who made all the advances. No doubt you saw the contentment on our good mother's face; how she caressed her; how she called her her dear daughter; how she would not let her leave her side? You no doubt saw how that good and beautiful Demoiselle caressed Christine and Marianne, and how she paid them pretty compliments; and how our father heard them with a joyful and satisfied look on his face, he who does not willingly put up with all those little pleasantries. When Mademoiselle Manon asked you why she had not seen Ursule, how did you react? A languorous look, and that was your response; and nevertheless she was contented. She even responded to our father for you, who asked you the same question. Do you know that I found you quite changed? You are always so frank, your letters are the proof of it; but you did not seem like that anymore. It is the city's influence apparently, and that is not your fault. O my Edmond! be as you were; don't ever change, my Edmond; when one is good, one can only change for the worse. I am a rustic, myself; I am coarse; but having remained virtuous, you see, I want to be a good brother, a good husband, a good son, and one day a good father. These are the sweetnesses that I owe to Marie-Jeanne. I never praise her appearance; even if there were no mirrors around, a women would always know better than anyone else what she possesses that is pretty; but I take her hand, and I do not kiss it, not like you do at any rate; instead, I say to her: "Marie-Jeanne, you seem so attentive to me, you will make a good wife when we are married; you love your father and your mother, you will love those who will come from you, and they will love you a lot, and you will raise them to be good people: we will always be in agreement, for you are gentle, and I am not disagreeable; everything redounds to me in you, Marie-Jeanne, from head to foot; it is not that you are prettier than any other; but you are proper, and everything suits you; you are a little fussy when it comes to eating, but so much the better, your family will be better nourished: you would never dream of beating a dog, you will raise your children gently, by reprimands tempered by kindness, and you will encourage them to act properly by that little gracious smile that you wear at the moment: you are somewhat devout; that is quite fine; I cannot be, myself; but I love the good God, and I pray to him every morning and evening, for my father, my mother, my brothers and sisters, for myself finally, and I will not forget you; you do not love the Priests; you are right; a woman must look at them without speaking to them, and speak to them without looking at them; which means, to see them at the altar, and speak to them at confession; so that, finally, Marie-Jeanne, we will get along quite fine together, we two." With these last words, I leave her, and I see her when I go, who looks at me as much as she can; and if I turn completely around to look at her, she lowers her eyes, and grows completely bashful. All that would seem like nothing to you anymore, now, you who have tasted the fine things the city has to offer; and your fine sensibility flinches in our small countryside. As for you, my Edmond, your happiness seems great and beautiful to me; and the only important thing now is to merit it; and that is what I hope for you. I encourage you to inform me about everything, and above all about these little schemes of Madame Parangon's, which I don't see the point of; unless it is that I suspect some duplicity by Tiennete. Above all remember that your wife will mean more to you than any male or female friend in the world. I forgot to say something about the good Father d'Arras: make sure that he is your friend, you understand me, and not your wife's; when women are like Mademoiselle Manon, it disturbs the meditations of a Monk, however pious he might be; go to see him at his place, and not he at yours; that's what I wanted to say. Adieu, my dear brother: write before and after you are married, to your good friend, for life.

XXVIII.

October 19.

Edmond to Pierrot.

He has the presentiments of some deceit.

During a violent storm, my dear older brother, the branches of a walnut tree planted on the top of a hill are less agitated than my mind and my heart; secret presentiments already prevented me from giving myself over to joy when I saw you under the arbor. It seems to me that everything is arranged for me in a different way than with other marriages. My parents arrived on Friday, I had a bann on Sunday, and on Tuesday I will be married by dispensation. Our father and mother have barely the time to speak a word with me; they are consumed by Father d'Arras, or by M. Parangon, or by M. Gaudet. Our brothers and sisters who have just arrived are put up in a pretty house in the suburb, belonging to the mother of my betrothed, but they can see nobody but Madame Palestine's family; what is more, Madame Parangon is nowhere to be found; her husband made her depart for the country; she brought Ursule with her, and our dear mother and father have stopped asking to see this Lady, and their daughter, as they did for the first two days; Tiennete even accompanies her mistress. There is something in all this that unsettles and troubles me; from the moment that my dear Manon leaves me to myself, I fall into an almost insurmountable melancholy... Need I admit to you that your manner of loving, both you and Marie-Jeanne, makes me jealous? I have before my eyes, while writing to you, that charming girl, who will soon be my sister: I tell her that I am writing to you... I must encourage her to add a word in her own hand... She does not dare to. O what lovely pudor! She refuses to write one word, although I assure her that it will make my letter more precious to you; but my mother has just entered the room, and she commands her to do it: read then, dear brother, what your future wife says, and kiss these cherished lines:

> *PIERRE, excuse me if I dare to write to you, but it is your good mother who wanted me to, and I do it purely out of obedience. You are all alone at present, and you have all the responsibility of the family on your shoulders: take care of yourself, I entreat you, for I know how you are, and how you work yourself to death. Your good mother is no longer there to see whether you are warm when you arrive home, to give you a glass of wine, and to make you change [your clothes]. It is perhaps improper for me to say too much; but if I am fine with being told to write these lines to you, it is mostly because I have the occasion to send them to you. Bye for now, Pierre, and I wish you good weather; for that makes the work less rough by half.*

– MARIE-JEANNE C***.

I was thinking, my friend, that her note would be sweeter... Ah! but what am I saying? In what terms would it need to be written that it might be more obliging! She only talks about you!

* * *

Father d'Arras arrived and I had to break this off; he led us all to take a walk; then he conducted us to his convent, and the women entered the garden with the Guardian's permission; we were served a bite to eat. I am, in truth, confused by all his kindnesses. He is supposed to dine with us this evening. He told us a thousand things in favor of my betrothed; and we listened to him with such great pleasure. On our return, he spoke to me in particular, and he engaged me in conversation about things that I had always envisaged from a very different point of view. It was a question of jealousy; he cited the customs of certain peoples, which are entirely unusual; and he seasoned those historical traits with such palpable reasons that I felt that what he said made good sense, although it still repulsed me a little. (M. Gaudet, who is very knowledgeable, and who has a marvelous library, promised to loan me the work that the Father was citing. During this conversation, and as we were traversing the road from Seignelai (where Madame Parangon is, with Ursule and Tiennete), a young man passed close by us; he looked at me as if he recognized me, and as he was riding away, he turned around two or three times to look back at me again. I was on the verge of following him, to put some questions to him, but the consideration that I owe to Father d'Arras restrained me. On our return, my betrothed came to fetch our mother and sisters, and she led them to her mother's place. I took advantage of that moment to finish this letter, and to reflect in solitude; for I have need of a little reflection.

XXIX.

The following day.

THE SAME TO THE SAME.

He discovers the deceit they want to practice.

Read, my brother, read, and if you can, control your indignation; as for myself, I abandon myself to all the feelings that my rage can inspire... Read:

LETTER FROM MADAME PARANGON TO
EDMOND.

The time for dissimulation is over, Monsieur; silence, under the circumstances that I know you to be in, would be a crime for me. You are being deceived; they want to dishonor you: Manon (keep this a secret between us), Manon is pregnant... she is pregnant... by my husband. And that is the reason for the haste which, doubtless, must have surprised you. I was kept at a distance because I was informed, and because it is well known how much of an interest I take in you. Nobody asks about Ursule now because of my conduct towards her, and our intimate friendship makes them presume I hide nothing from her. Tiennete, whom I have disguised so that she might reach you, must tell you the rest; believe this estimable girl; she will reveal to you all that she knows about Manon, because I tell her to. But keep this between us; do not dishonor my cousin in the mind of your parents; I want to save you and not lose her. I reserve for you a more advantageous arrangement, for a time more suitable to your establishment; I am sure of it. Let this sweet hope put your mind to rest. I love you, you and your sister, as much as myself. Stay well, my dear Edmond. Ursule embraces you. Do all that Tiennete tells you; but do not trust a certain M. Gaudet, Manon's cousin, who, if he had honest intentions, would not try to hide from me as he does.

My dear brother, just now, as I was exiting alone, the young man that I saw passing earlier, and who was apparently seeking to introduce himself to me, left this note for me. He said he would come and find me tomorrow, in the early morning, at the Arquebuse. It is Tiennete, and I did not recognize her! Adieu. I send you this letter, with that of yesterday's, by the regrater, who departs immediately. Until tomorrow when I will tell you the rest.

XXX.

THE SAME TO THE SAME.

He is disabused with respect to Tiennete, and recognizes whom he saw with his master in her clothing that day.

Happy older brother, the respectable Marie-Jeanne keeps you safe from the perils that I have just run, and which I still shudder to think about. Yesterday, at six o'clock in the morning, I was at the Arquebuse. I found there the young man, or rather Tiennete. With a glum attitude, a distracted eye, I advance, surrounded by a cloud of shame. – "How's that! such dejection for the loss of an object that you did not love!" said Tiennete, approaching me. I looked at her with surprise. "No, you did not love her," she repeated; "her youth and her coquetry blinded you; that is all. Believe me, you love another... Come, let us speak in private; let us pass behind this double hedge, where we will not be interrupted... I have read your heart, Edmond; for a long time now you have grown cold towards me. You have conceived injurious suspicions; but my self-interest alone could never have engaged me to try to dissipate them, to tell you a tale of wickedness and infamies... I need to start from the beginning.

TIENNETE'S STORY

I am from d'Aval, as you know. When M. Loiseau's father left Clam** in order to set himself up in our city, he had two sons and one daughter; this* *last person became my friend, and was the reason for all the problems that I had. On seeing the sister every day, I did not fail to become familiar with her older brother. This young man had received the best education; he had always lived in the world, either in Dijon, or in Paris; despite his youth, he was the tutor of the son of a president [of council] in the first of these two cities. His pupil died, and he returned to his paternal home. A character filled with gentleness, a sensitive heart, pure mores, set him apart from other men his age; my father and my mother welcomed him; but at the time when our hearts were already bound, without our even realizing it, Thérèse Loiseau had a dishonorable affair with an accounting clerk. He was a libertine, who distanced himself [from her] as soon as he knew of the state his credulous lover was in. You know how things are in our small towns: my parents, and particularly my father, forbade me from seeing anyone from that family. I will confess, to my shame, that I did not have the strength to obey him; they had some suspicions about us, and they made up their minds without telling me in advance, that I was to marry the first person who asked for my hand. I had no in-*

tentions of marrying anyone; but when I would have been more disposed to submission, it was the most hateful of men who presented himself. I found out about it indirectly, and I resolved to run away, not to give myself to M. Loiseau, but to avoid what I abhorred. Far from applauding my decision, my lover fought against my decision at first, and did not yield except by necessity.

After having left my father's house, I spent one week in a distant village, where I feigned to be ill; I was waiting, in order to depart, the signal that M. Loiseau was going to give to me, after those who had been on my track had returned home. When I arrived in this city, I was unknown to everyone, just as everyone was unknown to me. I went down to an obscure inn, whose owner, one Tourangeot, had been a Tartar[20] in the army, and who was then a domestic of M. Parangon's, who had always greatly loved him; I will tell you also that, by an unusual token of affection, he had him marry a servant-mistress of his, whom he had loved before his marriage. I said to the hostess (the same woman who had belonged to M. Parangon) that I had

---

[20]Original footnote: an officer's valet.

come to enter into her service. From the moment I had made this overture, which my clothing and my behavior hardly corroborated, many liberties were taken with me. In the evening, I wanted to go to bed early; I was told to wait a while, that I would sup at the table d'hôte; I saw no strangers there, so I consented; but as we were going to sit down to table, I saw a man from town enter, who was much welcomed. He said he would join us, and he took his place beside me. It did not take me long to realize that I was being taken for a loose woman; I grew confused, and as soon as I heard the loose language, I wanted to rise and retire to my room. M. Parangon (for it was he) took me into his arms and held me. I struggled with such courage that I escaped, and I avoided his impudent caresses. Imagine the situation that I found myself in! The host and hostess ridiculed me for my fears and my savage temperament; they added, coarsely, that I did not seem like someone who had always been so stubborn; that, furthermore, nobody would say anything more about it to me. I asked for my room, crying. I thought I saw M. Parangon make a sign to them to lead me to my room. I was trembling all over in that cursed house. Fortu-

nately, they had given me, for light, a lamp full of oil; I resolved to stay awake all night, and to barricade myself in my room. My precaution was not unreasonable. At eleven o'clock in the evening, I heard a small sound alongside the ruelle. I shrunk back in fright; but then, no longer hearing anything, I had the courage to go there in order to reassure myself with my eyes. On pulling aside the curtain, I found myself seized by two vigorous arms, and the lamp fell out of my hands. I let out a piercing cry; nothing could stop the miserable miscreant, who carried me to the bed, where, by the most indignant violence, he overcame my strength. At that very instant, someone knocked loudly on the ordinary door to the room; the brute who was holding me fled through the hidden door beside the ruelle. I was physically exhausted; I could barely sit up. It is what saved me; I had time to reflect. My first step was to bolt the secret door; then I declared that I would not open it for whoever it might be, until I glimpsed the light of day, because that depraved character who had attacked me had escaped, and because I had provided for my safety by locking the doors from within. I remained for some time without re-

sponding, and I thought I heard two people who were whispering to themselves: finally, the hostess raised her voice to ask me if I was dreaming or if my terrors were real; she exhorted me seriously to sleep, and then retired. Nothing else happened to me for the remainder of the night. The following morning, I descended at eight o'clock, after I had heard a lot of people stirring in the house. I asked to pay, in order to change lodgings. The hostess offered apologies, saying that everything that had happened to me was merely a test; that she saw quite well now that I was an honest girl, and that, in order to show me that she too was an honest woman, and to destroy the regrettable impression of the night before, she was going to procure a position for me, something that she would not have dared to do the night before. – "And to ensure you have no mistrust," she added, "here is the address; go there and present yourself to the Lady of the house; inform yourself in advance on her renown throughout the town, if you like, and you will hear what others have to say." – I took the address in hand, and I had reason to be satisfied by the information that I gathered; to the effect that my stay at that house, which should have been my undoing, was exactly its opposite. I presented myself at Madame Parangon's place; she was indeed in need of a girl; her husband's conduct had obliged her to send away the girl that came before me; I convinced her; but later she told me that it was with trepidation that she settled on me. And this is the first part of my story; now I pass to the second.

My astonishment was not mediocre when I served the table, to find that same bourgeois man, with whom I had supped at the tavern the night before, as the master of the house; I did not know yet how to disguise my feelings, and in my first feeling of fright, I thought I needed to tell my mistress everything. That virtuous woman responded to me: "My child, you must be prudent; you must not reveal everything; you could have conducted yourself with more wisdom in this case, and have left me ignorant of my husband's deviant acts; but now that the harm is done, the only thing I can do about it is to profit by it as much as I can. I count on you, Tiennete; you seemed honest to me from the start, and better educated than most girls of your station; I expect more from you consequently. Try to be with me for a long time; I would have known only one person who served me, if... you are delightful; I will be most pleased to employ you, and I hope the feeling will be reciprocated." – So much kindness penetrated me; I felt ready to open my heart to her; I took one of her hands, I kissed it, and my tears began to flow. – "My child," she said to me, "I do not know what to think!... would it be you then who would be... get up; a certain presentiment tells me that you are worthy of my friendship; but let us get to know each other first; prudence demands it." – She left me, because someone had arrived; and when I was later alone with her, that incomparable woman, who had heard tell of my adventure, and who had recognized me in part, did not ask a single question of me in order to instruct herself completely.

Several days passed without M. Parangon paying any attention to me. That apparent calm did not last. One day, when Madame was dining with her aunt Canon, he came to find me in his wife's apartments. At first, he employed the most seductive promises, and advantageous offers; then he said to me that if I changed his love into hatred because of a refusal, I could very well repent my mistake. I responded that I had nothing to be afraid of by doing my duty. Since he had entered, I always kept my eye on the door, in order to escape, and to leave him alone; but his position blocked my passage. Finally, by a movement that he made, in order to come closer to me, I succeeded in escaping, and I remained in the salon where everyone passed by, until Madame returned. He was furious with me; for I did not want to perform any orders that he gave me and which exposed me to a situation where I would fall into his hands.[21] He complained to his wife when she returned: my mistress pretended great astonishment, scolded me a little, and begged him to forgive me. But when we were alone, she said to me; "I see quite clearly, my child: you are made for me: do not say anything about M. Parangon; but tell me about yourself: who are your parents?" – I blushed at this question. – "Are you afraid," she resumed, "to confide your secrets in me?" – "Me, Madame!?" I replied to her; "Ah! you will know everything..." Indeed, I confessed to her everything that I just related to you. She found fault with the boldness and inconsideration of my decisions; but with such

---

[21]Original footnote: This is what the original had: *For I did not want to go water the white chicory in the cellar, etc.*

restraint that I sensed her goodness more than her reproof. I showed her a letter by M. Loiseau, who was supposed to arrive in several days, of his parents' vow, with all the precautions necessary to avoid giving any suspicion of our correspondence. – "And from now on, my child," Madame Parangon said to me, "you will prove to me that you are worthy of my esteem, by never seeing your lover alone; must I have you give me your word?" I did not hesitate to promise her it; and I did not fail to keep my word, except once, and for important reasons that obliged me; it was not even a tryst, for I only said one word to him, to engage him to come immediately into a house where his presence was needed. M. Loiseau arrived: my good mistress saw him, and she approved of my choice: she did even more, she took it upon herself to calm my parents, showing them that I was in an honest house whose mistress, having become my friend, would be a sufficient caution for my conduct, from the moment that Lady wanted to make herself known. I added several lines in my own hand to that letter; I begged them a thousand pardons for my false conduct, and I promised them, before God, never to do anything that would be unworthy of their blood, and of the education they had given me. I learned from M. Loiseau that my parents had shown the letter to everybody, and that it had greatly diminished the bitterness of their sorrow.

It was under these circumstances that the death of a very rich relative, whom she was the sole inheritor of, obliged Madame to go to Paris. As soon as she heard the news, she called me to her: "My child," she said to me, "it would not be prudent of me to leave a tender lamb under the teeth of the famished wolf: I am about to depart, what will we do? If I bring you with me, he will know the reason; if I leave you, I expose you to him: I would like to find a way not to show mistrust, but to keep you safe..." She reflected for a moment: "I think I have found it," she added; "my cousin Manon is a sensible girl, even though quite young, and she knows how to deal with my husband, when he gets it into his head to act freely; I will engage her to stand in for me during my absence; you will never leave each other's side, and M. Parangon won't dare to make an attempt on either of you... I will see to all this... Yes," she continued, "this is the only reasonable course of action; I am almost at ease now. Manon is a bit haughty; you will likely have to suffer a bit... I will have a few words with her; but keep our secret between us; in the situation that you find yourself in, overly marked good manners would be dangerous, because it would draw attention to you." Everything transpired according to Madame's plan.

My respectable friend departed. How I wept!... Mademoiselle Manon made friends with me in the first few days, and we were inseparable; but gradually I saw her change and she grew cold; she began to leave me alone, against her promises to Madame. One day M. Parangon profited by it to renew his vile propositions to me; he dared to corner me, and to allow himself to speak loose language to me, which he forced me to listen to. I do not know to what purpose he came to tell me that the man who had tormented me in the inn sought only to procure himself an easy triumph; and that if I had opened the door, when someone knocked, under the pretext of coming to my aid, he would not now be reduced to desiring a thing that he would have enjoyed then and there. During his discourse, he employed a ruse; he told me, while laughing, that in any case I could not escape now. My situation frightened me; I defended myself in desperation; my cries sur-prised him, but did not put him off; he strove to make them stop by a method worthy of him. He succeeded, and my indignation, while redoubling my ef-forts, exhausted my forces, until I heard Mademoiselle Manon, out of breath, crying to open the door. M. Parangon hastened to set things right as best he could. He opened the door. Mademoiselle entered furiously; I broke out into tears. She heaped re-proaches on her cousin; she dared to tell me that I just received what I had desired. – "No, Mademoiselle," I cried, "I did not desire it, any more than I sought it; no, thank God, and you; although you treat me so severely now, I am nonetheless obliged to you. But I am going now; I will not stay here one more moment." – I quickly went downstairs. Mademoiselle Manon ran after me. She represented to me that I was going to make a re-grettable scene; and that I ought to wait for Madame Parangon, and do as she believed best. She had no difficulty persuading me, my heart told me as much. Where to find a mistress, a friend, like Madame? I retired to a small room in the house where I wept bitterly the sad effects of my having run from my parents' home; until then,

I had thought it excusable; but the consequences that it had already produced, and those that it had yet to produce, made me appreciate the full extent of my temerity.

*From this time on, M. Parangon no longer said a word to me. Calmness was restored in my heart; Mademoiselle Manon's coldness towards me visibly increased; I paid it no attention; the most marked disdain ensued; she insisted on vilifying me. What did I care about all that? My true mistress esteemed me; she deigned to write to me. I no longer spoke with M. Loiseau; but I saw him, I was tranquil, almost without remorse. It was around this time that you arrived, M. Edmond. I saw in you, from the very first day, a young man to be esteemed by his moral behavior, made for being the friend of M. Loiseau and me. You had even other claims to my heart; it was Madame who had sounded out your parents through a bailiff of V***; she had seen you one day on the road to S***, when you were leading your father's flock to the river, in order to have them bathed; she was charmed by your conversation with the young village girls who accompanied you; she informed herself of you; and on the responses she received, she de-*

sired to draw you out of the village, and she spoke to M. her father about it. As you can imagine, she was quite upset to be absent when you arrived: she wrote me to take good care to compensate you for everything that you might have suffered; and that will help explain to you my behavior with respect to you. But, on the other hand, your delightful candor had an unexpected effect on M. Parangon and on Madame's cousin (even if they hadn't informed you about the plans they have for you today). The disdain that this latter person showed you was merely affectation; it was a consequence of M. Parangon's counsels, whom experience had only too well taught that obstacles make objects more desirable. Mademoiselle Manon felt a growing liking for you; she made no mystery of it to me one day when she was in a bad mood, and let me see that she feared me as a rival. I felt compelled to reassure her. But what was the effect of that growing liking for you?... Read this note: do you recognize the hand in which it is written?

You need to put an end, charming cousin, to the rigors as well as to everything else: I did not wish to say it to you this morning, however much I wanted to,

for fear of seeing your beautiful eyes fill with anger; but I
write it to you; and as I am going to dinner in town, you will
have time to reflect on it before
my return. Also, if Tiennete
was distracting me again from
the adoration I owe your
charms, is it not your fault?
You should have let me the
other day, and already I would
no longer be thinking about it. I
believe even that it is not her
whom I desire; it is her pinched
waist; that simple and charming manner of dress, so dull
looking on other girls of her
sort, so appetizing, so cute on
her, – wear it, cousin; I had one
made for you from the same
stuff, a prettier one than Tiennete's, under the pretext of a
ball; have the complaisance to
put it on; you will efface that
girl. How cute you will look!...
No, my little tease, I love nobody else but you: my beautiful
indolent wife, with her eighteen years of age, and her big
wild eyes, has never inspired in
me half of what I feel for you:
your vivacity, your little trans-
ports, your resistance, it is all

so charming. Ah! my dear Manon, you are a treasure!... Abjure then that fatal reserve, which has ruined everything to date; fear no more, my little chicken, the usual bogeyman of girls, for we have a plan all ready to repair your honor, if I should make a visible breach in it; a dupe has been found... My faith, the epithet does not fit him; he is young, but not a fool; but he could be, one day, in a certain way, after he has served our designs. The most pleasant thing of all is that he is my wife's protégé; in any case, you can be quite sure that I will do even more for him than I have promised, because of you, my charming cousin. Adieu, Poupon; I will see you again in three hours, a bit gay, but no more than is needed for love.

(Such was, my poor brother, the note that I read; it is quite certainly written by M. Parangon, it is his hand alright: o, the infamy!...)

Read this other one, said Tiennete to me:

You want me to comply with your every wish, imperious cousin... eh, well, I consent;

but... on the condition that you vouch for your pupil and Mama's consent, and that you will commit to nothing that you cannot deliver on. For my part, in order to show you that I intend only to treat you in the same manner, I send you this note by the Fixer; the sauce will be spicy for you. As for the seasoning you propose for me, I am all the more ready for it, for I see by this means how to destroy Tiennete in the young man's mind. You need only act with due precaution in order to be seen in a way that does not compromise me.

(Oh! the indignant creature! I was speechless... I now recall having delivered it, that abominable note!... Tiennete continued.)

And there you have M. Parangon and his lovely cousin: they are unmasked by these two notes, which Madame and I would have been quite hesitant to show to a young man less prudent than you. But we counted greatly on your sense of moderation, believing that you would leave it to Madame the trouble of delaying and then finally breaking off this marriage. Your sister knows everything; it is she who, at the right time and place, must inform your parents. Do you permit me now, after asking you a question, to bring you up to speed on things? Do you understand what we have proposed to show you? – I responded that I understood. – Eh! What then did you think of me? – "Things," I said, turning red in the face, "that I ask your pardon for." And at this moment, having reflected that I had a watch on me, which I felt I came by unworthily, I took it out, exclaiming that I was going to smash it. – Oh no, no, Tiennete said to me, holding my hand back; really, you need not do that for my benefit... In order to convince you to keep it without hesitation, I must tell you, that things are not what you think... On leaving my parents' home, I had a small amount of gifts that had been given to me since my childhood; I had kept them in tact for the most part; one day, you will express much admiration for M. Loiseau's watch... you are his friend and, I dare say, mine: I begged Madame to bring it and give it to you... without any qualms on my part; you know how pure the gifts of friendship are; and something that should make this gift dear to you is knowing that it is worth twice the value of what remains; a person worthy of all our respectful attachment has furnished the rest. But let's get back to what I had to say to you.

The two criminal lovers did not burn, as they should have done, the notes that you have just read. M. Parangon left his on his cabinet, with other papers, and forgot about it: Mademoiselle Manon had given him back the other one, or he had taken it back. Around the same time, Madame having written to me, asking me to send her some baskets of fruit and game, I had need of some papers to arrange all that; I asked M. Parangon for them; and in those that he told me to grab, the two notes were found by chance. I did not see them; the baskets arrived in Paris, and Madame threw these papers away without looking at them: the people with whom she was staying saw them, and spoke to her about them in veiled terms; these people moreover did not know Mademoiselle Manon, and did not suspect that it was she who has running the household. But, after Madame had returned home, they thought they should send her the two letters. Imagine her surprise when she recognized her husband's handwriting and that of her cousin! As for myself, I had observed several indications of a criminal com-

merce between Monsieur and Mademoiselle Manon; but I did not believe I needed to say anything to Madame. On her return, she saw through her husband's plans with respect to you, by means of several conversations that she overheard between him and Mademoiselle Manon. She was horrified, and it is only since then that she no longer sees her cousin in a good light; she almost forgave her the one foible; but she could not excuse so dark a deception; you interest her immensely, I want to acknowledge this on her behalf; but even if you meant nothing to her, were hateful to her even, she would never allow an honest young man to be deceived in the disgraceful manner that they propose. That a certain Tourangeot, a vile soul, should have married his master's concubine, knowing full well what he was getting himself into, he had a valid reason for doing so in such a man's eyes: personal interest; but you, M. Edmond, who have a bright future, if you know how to merit it, you would become the detestable veil that hides a criminal intrigue!... No, you will not be so demeaned... Assuage your grief; dry your tears, which ought only to be for shame for having been played. Madame has in mind a plan that will give you neither regrets, nor confusion: an even more beautiful young person... – "Would that be Edmée?" I interrupted her with emotion – To be honest, that lovely person would be more than capable of compensating you for your pain; but if I can believe certain words that escaped our charming mistress, it is someone even better. You must not see her for a while, the person that she destines for you: she plans to place her with the dear Ursule, and under the watch of Madame Canon, in a respectable house in the Capital, where Madame is cherished: they will both be taken in, without danger to their moral behavior, and those graceful airs that captivate you. When she made you conceal the arrival of your sister, she hardly anticipated that everything would turn out as it did, and that your parents were on the verge of arriving: but according to her new arrangement, Ursule must make an appearance this afternoon, and Madame will strive to have your father and mother approve it; she thinks only of your benefit, the two of you; it is the aim of all her endeavors. A powerful motive drives her to it. – "Eh, what is that?" – Madame has no children; she is almost certain never to have any; she will consider you like a brother: it is a personal bias that nothing will change; M. Parangon made a settlement on you, conditional to your marriage contract with Mademoiselle Manon, of the greatest part of his property, in the event that he should not have children: Madame will do even better than that, and if death should take her, you would be her only legatee, and her family could do nothing about it even if they wanted to. Love her then like a tender sister; she has all the feelings of a sister for you. Far from being carried away by jealousy like her cousin, her sincerest desire with regard to her husband would be that he attach himself to that girl, because she too has started to grow attached to him; M. Parangon would take care of his health thereby, he would avoid crazy outlays, and all the consequences of libertinage; she herself would find some tranquillity: for she repeats it often enough, that happiness is no longer in the cards for her; it is tranquillity alone that she aspires to. I must leave you now: moderate your emotions; dissimulate; obey Madame: if someone calls on you this afternoon, go out, and do everything that you are told to do.

Eh, well, my brother?... Oh! what dangerous back alleys these cities are made of, just as I was starting to grow so fond of them! And there you have my dignant master! what wickedness!... what a trap for simplicity that vile corrupter of innocence lays!... I want my mother, and my sisters, to leave here immediately; the impure air that one breathes here would sully them; Marie-Jeanne, after a longer sojourn, would become less worthy of my brother. But what am I saying! Madame Parangon, or rather virtue itself, – does she not live here? O place of contradictions, and terrible chaos, when will you sort yourself out for me!...

I write to you while waiting for the others to rise from bed. My friend, come find our parents and your mistress; run; feign adversity; make up a lie, for the first time in your life; Ursule, who will appear, will reveal everything to our mother along the way, and she will sever my unjust bonds. Adieu.

End of Part One.

Part Two

XXXI.

Pierrot to Edmond.

Women love the city.

Our family is back home now, my Edmond; and a letter from Madame Parangon, which Ursule delivered, informs our mother and father of everything; but we are so troubled and embarrassed that we scarcely know how to hide it; for everyone asks us if you are married; and our sisters and Marie-Jeanne, if they danced at your wedding; and we respond as best we can. It is still a lot better, however, than saying that you were so villainously had. And I can no longer believe what I am about to say to you: I should have praised what I blamed, and blamed what I praised. Our father and mother are in a state of chagrin; and if you will, I see the moment when they would be totally ready to change their minds, and take you back home again: I only await your response to speak with them about it. As far as Ursule is concerned, they no longer want her to return to the city: and it would take Madame Parangon already to convince her, for she does not seem happy, and I refuse to believe that the city pleased her after only two days; that said, one should not swear to anything; according to what little I've seen, cities are made for women, and just as Messire Antoine Foudriat, our Curate, said one day, they are the element that women need; once they have gotten a taste for it, when one tries to remove them from it, they are like a fish out of water. But getting back to you, my Edmond, act prudently, so as not to make any enemies; listen to the counsels of the good Father d'Arras and M. Gaudet. Ursule is discreet; she has said nothing to me because she does not suspect that I have been kept up to date; and our other brothers and sisters know nothing. I embrace you with a truly fraternal heart, and look forward to seeing you soon among us again; if that is your wish however.

XXXII.

November 1.

EDMOND TO PIERROT.

This is the first letter in which sincerity is largely lacking.

My dear older brother, I will not experience the happiness of living in the countryside again; the die is cast; I love the city and at the same time I detest it; but I feel that I cannot leave it; it is an impossible thing, at present, and I am here for good. In fact, you see me retained by a thousand ties, all so strong that nothing can break them. If I seek the cause of my liking for the city, I find it in the politesse, more agreeable than cordiality; in the graciousness of manners; our elegant people of the countryside are merely ridiculous here; it happens thereby that one grows insensibly accustomed to rising above them; there is more to it than that: a city man who spends some time in the country seems, on his return, to recognize the superiority of city folk; he seems more timid, less assured, until he has caught back up on things. Whence, that invincible repugnance that one finds in all those who have gotten a taste for the city, to return to the countryside and debase themselves; to leave behind the role of a polished man of the city, and the airs that suit him, in order to revert to the title of a country person and to participate in the ignobility that is its varnish. You cannot believe how a motive so weak in appearance retains young people without their suspecting that so small a thing determines them. But add to that also that the stay is more pleasant, the objects more agreeable, the faculty of thinking finer and more developed here. (And this is an important point, my friend, for the same manner of thinking is shared, and as soon as one has gotten the hang of it, one finds enjoyment only with those who share it; one disdains others; one is tired of his superiority.) You will tell me that city people are more spiteful; I leave them to you; but the reasons I gave you are fortified by another, which has its origin in the most natural and finest penchant; it is that the women here are beautiful flowers, species of bewitching sirens, who provide a thousand different kinds of pleasures; at home, one senses merely the physical aspect of love (in other words, the pleasures of the senses); with the exception of some delicate hearts, such as your own, my brother, tenderness is hardly known there; but here, the physical aspect of love and tenderness are merely one part in a hundred of the known delights that women procure. There are young people here who are happy as soon as they have shown themselves [in public] and the beautiful young ladies of the city have seen them pass and repass along the promenade; they know that this pleasure is reciprocated and that those whom they wish to be seen by, desire to see and be seen; if they are greeted by a pretty woman, it is a glory that swells their heart, and fills it in the most pleasing manner in the world. The society of the beautiful sex here is charming; the conversation of women is seductive; their manners have an easiness about them, a lightness, so many graces, that time flies when one is with them, in a continual intoxication. You have no idea, my friend, the feelings that are stirred in a man's heart by the obliging smile of a pretty person, a single word, a gesture of familiarity in front of a bevy of rivals, and a thousand other things that I don't dare mention, for fear that this subject matter is not to your liking. I return to your offer, and I thank you for it, as a proof of your friendship; but I do not want to take you up on it; so do not ask me anymore about a recourse that would not make me happy; anymore, I almost do not deserve anymore to live among you; and if you love me so much as all your behavior towards me has shown thus far, grant me something that I fervently desire in compensation, employ everything you have to bring Ursule back to me; her presence is necessary to me, her views will be useful, her society will keep me from having to search for others', and we will mutually sustain each other.

I feel calm enough today to continue telling you in detail everything that you do not know.

As soon as Tiennete left me, I returned to my room to reflect on what my next step would be. After a thousand resolutions, each one destroyed by the one that followed it, I decided to let Madame Parangon act. At the hour when I was to visit Mademoiselle

Manon at her mother's place, I showed up as usual. I found her more beautiful, tender, interesting than ever; at that moment, she eclipsed every lovely thing I knew... I lowered my eyes, my heart palpitated; I regretted... I regretted that she no longer seemed worthy of my attachment. I told myself that I was experiencing a vain joy that was going to vanish at any moment like smoke into thin air! Manon! Manon!... She excited desires from the bottom of my heart; her baseness did not prevent them from being born; I felt even a more vivid prodding; I have no idea what nature that feeling was made of; doubtless, it was not pure, for I blushed a moment later because of it; I felt it again, and shame immediately followed. I believe that that there is the beginning of crime; for I was telling myself that she will not be my wife, that I would rather die than suffer her to become my wife; and yet, I desired her! And there you have it, what was passing through my mind when I approached her. I did not say one word to her: she led me into a particular room. – "You are quiet today," she said to me, taking my hand; "Look at me? I see anxiety in your eyes, what is wrong?... what has happened, my dear husband?" – She said it in such a caressing tone of voice, that I could not hold back the tears. Oh! what tears! I have never cried such bitter ones. If I had not written anything to you, if Madame Parangon did not know anything, I would have thrown myself into her arms, and I would have exclaimed, "Manon, I know everything, and I forgive you." But it no longer depended on me. – "What is wrong?" she repeated; "my dear Edmond! you are frightening me!" – "Ah! Mademoiselle, I am quite miserable!" – "Heavens!" – "Mademoiselle, I loved you." – "What are you saying! You don't love me anymore then!" – "It must hardly matter to you." – "To me, great God! It hardly matters to me!?" – "Mademoiselle, you do not love me, you have never loved me..." – "Stop... Who told you that, ungrateful person?" – "Your behavior: my loss must hardly affect you: you have cruelly... Mademoiselle, what did I do to deserve... what interest did you have to pile infamy on a poor unfortunate... on you yourself even?" – "I allow you to speak; patiently, I allow you to insert the dagger." – "It was you who first plunged it into my heart." – "Ah! that's too much!... Edmond, I love you... I love you..." – "You might prove it to me." – "Yes, I will prove it to you. I could not imagine this cruel conversation... I could not imagine... I am lost!... Take this sheet of paper and read: all it needs now is your signature at the bottom of it, at the Notary's. You will read, then, this document; I was going to have it sent to you today even; the contents prove it, that I wanted to owe everything to your generosity. Edmond, I am faithful to you since the moment I loved you: and if by ill fortune before that, I... But read..."

I read it, dear brother; it was a document in which Manon's mother and sister gave all their property to me. Then I unsealed the paper that I am about to transcribe for you.

> *When you begin reading this humiliating confession, she who wrote it, who will die of grief if she cannot move you, will embrace your knees; and this posture suits her* (she had taken up that

posture, dear Pierrot; I could not endure it). *She would not have waited until now to reveal her heart to you, to make you the master of her secrets, if others' counsels, her inexperience, and the fear of losing you had not persuaded her against it. Yes, dear lover, my fate is in your hands; you can give me life or death, infamy or honor. I am lost without you; with you, I am happy (if someone can still be happy, even in the arms of the person she loves, with a heart shredded by remorse!). This document that I give to you, which I sign, in which I confess my guilt to you, which my mother and my sister have signed with me, would be either your assurance against lapses, which you can regard as impossible, or the certain justification for your vengeance, if in the future I should give you reason for complaint. I permit you to entrust it to that brother of yours in whom, it is said, you have all confidence, sealed however, so that I do not blush except in your eyes. O my dear lover! do not hate me; I am at your knees like a criminal who awaits a terrible sentence. Let yourself yield to the tears that I release...If I had not loved you, and you alone; if my tenderness for you did not make me prefer you to my happiness even, your lover could have resolved to try to deceive you perhaps. But she cannot live without you; another who offered his hand to her, inspired only separation and distance in her. It is you whom she wants, or death. Have pity on her despair... Another... o what sorrow! what an inextinguishable source of tears... But he did not have the first condition of her heart; would that the lover whom she adores might deign to believe her, totally unworthy though she is!*

Ready to unite myself to the man whom I will love forever, my conscience obliges me, in spite of the advice of my closest friends and family, to reveal to him,... that someone once triumphed over my virtue, and that I carry now the marks of my crime... But, if he is generous enough to forgive me, I hope to make it up to him so that one day he will have occasion to be glad for it: I adore him, he knows this; the ordinary duties of a wife will constitute for me merely a recompense; I want to extend those duties beyond the prescribed limits, and impose on myself a dependency that punishes me and rewards him. My mother and I, we want that this document should extend his rights, and that it give him an unlimited authority over my person; that he be made master, *from the moment he wishes, and without any other motive than his will, to oblige me to live either in the countryside, on a farm in Etivé, or in a convent, paying a pension, the most modest possible pension, against my property, which we will forfeit to him in all fairness. But if he have the indulgence to suffer me to live beside him, allowing me to love him, never will he see a more tender lover, more faithful, more attentive to please him, nor a wife more prompt to ensure his least desires. I entreat him to regard, as the first mark of my devotion, this document which I deliver unto him. Written in A***, this 22 October 17**.*

(Signed by the mother and two sisters.)

P.S. *I await my destiny, dear Edmond: say it: but alas! would that it might be indulgent.*

As soon as I had finished reading it, she rushed into my arms; she pressed me against her breast: I did not know where I was: she did not speak; but she wept; I wept too, more touched by her suffering than upset by her wrongs. I said to her finally: "Mademoiselle, I do not hate you; I do not despise you; but..." – "Pile your reproaches on me," she interrupted me; "I deserve them, dear Edmond: wield your power, abuse it, if you like, and know just how far my love will go." – "M. Parangon..." – "He has destroyed me, and you can save me: he is a monster in my eyes, I never want to see him again." – "You mocked me; you had me deliver a note..." – "I don't deny it... Dear lover, I was not changed yet, but it was not at all for the reasons given by those who have informed you about it (for I can guess who they are)." – "Ah! Manon, it was cruel of you to make me be the bearer..." – "Say the word, and I will avenge you, on myself and on my accomplice. You should know that that unworthy suborner plans to continue... after our union; that he loves me, and that I have eclipsed everything that is in his heart, and that he gives in to me only by an excess of tenderness; that feeling, which he does not believe is made for him, he experiences it, and it is the first time in his life he says; I wield it to dominate him and oblige him to serve us; he does so, all the while enraged, like those wicked spirits that the Divine Will forces to bend to the just, sometimes... My friend, if you knew how his infamous seduction was effected, you would excuse me a little perhaps... a small ray of hope remains for me... if you wished, you could help me win back my cousin's affection; she would be my only friend from then on; I would see her, but never her husband." – "My dear Manon, there is no more hope; you see me overwhelmed by the sorrow of losing you." – "No, my friend, your heart is not that hard; no... Come here, my lover; come here, my loving husband..." – She pressed herself up against me. We held each other in each other's arms for a long time; her beauty kept me; the sweetness of her caresses set my spirit free; it seemed as though she had rid it of the cruel incertitude that was constraining it previously; she made my soul joyful, she gave vivacity to my feelings... (O God! what felicity am I renouncing, I said to myself!) what are all the other beautiful things in the world compared to Manon, if not beautiful paintings, and admirable statues, that one would need, like Pygmalion,[22] to beg Love to animate with that divine fire that embellishes beauty. – "Will I be yours?" she said to me after a long silence. – "Manon! you are my divinity; you play on my irresolutions." – "I might have touched you!" – "You have done more than that." – "O good young man! your heart is pure, your soul is sensitive; I will not abuse it." – "Abuse it, if you like; Manon, my days, my honor, it is all yours." – "Let's go, my charming friend, let's run and tell my mother, that I owe my life to you! Come on, my spouse!"

We paid a visit to Madame Palestine; there, the various questions put to me left no doubt in my mind that I had not been informed of everything before Manon confessed to me. The Mother and two sisters looked at each other for a long time in silence; finally, Madame Palestine, addressing a word to me, said: "Would you consent that from now on we would go to Autel, if that were possible?" – "Whatever you would like," I responded: "I do not know whether I would be happy, but she told me that she would be happy, and that is enough for me." – Manon's expressions of thanks were so tender that they strengthened

---

[22]Original footnote: Pygmalion was a famous Sculptor who made so beautiful a statue that he fell in love with it; he begged Venus to animate it, and his prayer was answered. It is a trait of ancient Mythology that I am obliged to study for my art. (Note by Edmond himself)

me in my resolve. M. Parangon was announced; Manon begged her mother to keep us from his sight. In time, everything was made ready. M. Gaudet took the initial steps with me; we obtained the advancement that was asked for, and Father d'Arras was supposed to give us his blessing and consent in the presence of the Curate; everything was ready to be concluded; I was then wishing that he who came on your behalf to find our father and mother did not arrive. Nevertheless, our steps and our preparations had taken time; it was nearly eleven o'clock; my mother and sisters were standing beside my betrothed; the family had been alerted that for unforeseen circumstances we were obliged to hasten things, when an unknown young man, having slid up to Marie-Jeanne, urged her to inform me, in the strictest of confidence, that someone wanted to speak with me. I descended without anyone noticing; I was expecting to find Tiennete, and I was quite determined about what I had to say to her; it was not her. "What are you doing!" she said to me; "are you going to ruin yourself? What! You will be married, in spite of what you know?" By the sound of her voice, I knew it was Madame Parangon. – "Oh! Madame, it's you!" I cried. – "Come with me," she continued; "come and explain this inexplicable mystery to me: you are going to marry Manon?" – "I am more loved than she is blamable: ah! if you only knew her!" – "Too well!" – "She wants to be your friend, never to see your husband again." – "And she was able to seduce you!" – "If that's what it is, Madame, leave me to my error, she is dear to me; I love your cousin." – "Youth... (ah God! how inexperience is dangerous sometimes!)... youth and desires deceive you; you think that you are in love; come on, young man, you can trust me, just about everyone thinks in the same way, and repents it the next day; you see someone; they please you; you think they are suited for you; you marry; neither of you took the time to realize that you are mistaken; you are both enraged, but it is too late. Shudder, tremble at the mere suggestion of marriage; shiver, on imagining that she is the person you will give to yourself as an inseparable companion... Tell me, do you esteem her?" – "I love her; that is more than esteem." – "I pity you! it is a thousand times less." – "Madame, love fortifies all honest, obliging feelings..." – "Ah love, yes! but no: it is the charm produced by the advances and caresses of a coquette, which you fancy to call love." – "I am grateful to her." – "With good reason?" – "Yes, Madame, with good reason." – "In fact, you and I, we owe her a great deal; let us unite our gratitude, I beg you, she will see the most spectacular effect of it... Ah! you blush, Edmond, but not because of me, who am your friend, – but in your own eyes. Would you have said the same things in front of Ursule?" – "Madame, I do not see how..." – "Which would have prevented you. Ah! my poor Edmond, without me you were doomed then!... Someone loves you, you say! The effort is rare; it surprises me a great deal! Someone gives you their property (I am informed, as you can see): would such a small matter interest you? Is it not then because this match is financially beneficial to you?... Do you not see that she has wanted from the start to make you her dupe; that she has seen you from too close up, and that she herself has become the dupe of love (but I must not say yours)?

And then here you are, in the palm of her hand!... Father d'Arras (with good intentions of course) and M. Gaudet (with bad ones, surely) help to push you over the precipice; I render the former some justice; it is out of friendship for you; because, not knowing that someone has other, more advantageous plans for you, he believes that you do not have any other course to follow than the one that fortune presents to you at the moment; as for the latter, he would not be so delicate himself. A bachelor has no idea of a certain decency of moral behavior, which is known only by honest married men... Let's cut to the chase, Edmond: if you were loved by someone else, and more tenderly, and more disinterestedly, and by a more worthy, more beautiful, more tender, what do I know? a richer (but I do not insist on this point) person, what would you resolve?" – "Madame, Manon would die if I abandoned her: do you hear that commotion inside; the relatives are here; a noise is building; your family [is] anticipated: leave me to fulfill my fate; I would leave you to yourself." – "My astonishment has no bounds!... How blind you are! M. Gaudet drew up the document that you read; he dictated everything... You will not be the master of your ruin; no, you will not. Adieu. In a moment your sister comes to share her feelings for you." She left me. I just stood there, watching her walk away; she had disappeared, when I thought I could still hear her and speak with her...

In spite of myself, dear older brother, they managed to tear me away from my inclination. After a quarter of an hour, Ursule appeared; she conversed with our mother. He whom you sent did the rest. Our parents, apparently frightened by a trifle that was greatly exaggerated to them, after their having been informed of it,[23] cut the ceremony short and departed, leaving behind the prepared party, the signed contract, the parish registers even; Father d'Arras, ever provident, and M. Gaudet who is even more so, having engaged the redactor to keep the document ready, to avoid spending too much time at Church, given that the hour was already late. In one hour, all that numerous assembly had dissipated into thin air, and your brother found himself alone with Manon... Prudence sometimes abandons the wisest among us... But I say too much. Sometimes, in spring and autumn, the sky is covered with thick, moving clouds; the brilliant sunlight presents the image of a most beautiful day; then, darkened by a thick cloud, one would have thought it was sad December; such is my state.

Adieu my friend. Madame Parangon waits for Ursule, and she waits for her this week: while I owe you the satisfaction of seeing them reunited.

XXXIII.

Same day.

MANON TO M. GAUDET.

She seems changed.

My husband wrote to his older brother with a view to preparing from a distance a necessary consent, just as

---

[23]Original footnote: It had to do with a fire that broke out in a small lean-to that was full of straw, because of the imprudence of a tiller who had been there in the morning, before dawn, with a lamp.

you had advised us to do. Now I have a favor to ask of you, of you and Father d'Arras, after having expressed to you my warmest gratitude, however; for (and I will always acknowledge it) without the confession and devotion that you suggested to me as a last resort, after the manner in which you had disposed M. R***'s mind, without the information that you had given me as to my cousin's preparations, I was done for; I am indebted to you for much more than that; the fact of the matter is that the feelings you have inspired in me have become natural to me; they always guide my behavior. But I have a favor to ask: trust me that what I am about to say is only because of the perfect knowledge I have of your feelings: you are an atheist (I employ this term because I know that it does not offend you): in the name of... everything that is dear to you (for nothing is sacred to you, and that is the difficulty!) – do not try to destroy what you call prejudices in my Husband; I have been your accomplice; I cease to be it now; you know how I was raised; sooner or later, the good principles [of one's upbringing] take an upper hand; I recognize then that without the sentiments of Religion, honor, and restraint, there is no happiness in life; I abjure my wayward behavior; eh! would that my tears could erase the marks!... I am happy, but I did not deserve it; it is up to me to repair through my future behavior what the preceding behavior was guilty of; I hope that you will not reject it; and [accept that] I am of this persuasion, with gratitude, etc.

XXXIV.

RESPONSE.

May the oil of wickedness not anoint my head.

Carte blanche for everything that does not regard my belief, charming cousin; but you do me the greatest injustice if you think that I am without mores. I am thirty-two years old, and a person is formed by that time. Are you aware of any mistakes I have made? You know what I think about your sex: I fear it, I flee from it, and I adore it; the presence of women is a beneficial fire, which warms me and fills me with joy; but I stay at a comfortable distance in order not to feel anything more than a gentle warmth, and I would be quite upset if someone forced me to hold it in the palm of my hand, like another Scævola.[24] As for what is called love, I respect only the medicinal physic in suitable moderation. It is not the same for friendship; that is a feeling that I am more avid about than a person suffering from dropsy for the prohibited drink; and I do not know what it is about the naïve charm written all over Edmond's face, and in all his manners, that attracts me to him; I love him, and I admit that you owe acts of grace to my exemption of prejudices; for without that, you would have nothing, and I would have used him against you. Father d'Arras thinks like me as regards that amiable young man, and he is delighted to find me of the same disposition as himself. Tell us then what we need to do to make your husband happy, and we will do it. I swear to you

---

[24]Scævola: Caius Mucius Scævola (circa BC 507), an early hero of the Roman Republic. He is famous for having put his right hand into a fire and calmly said, "See how unimportant the body is to those who have only glory in mind." Consequently he earned the nickname Scævola which means left-handed.

by what is most dear to me; by my young friend.

XXXV.

November 15.

EDMOND TO PIERROT.

This here is a trap that he lays for us.

My dear older brother! Is anyone at home thinking about us! What is going on? Nothing has been said to Madame Palestine, nothing written!... Wasn't some-one supposed to be managing things in such a way that the rupture happened without openly shocking anyone? Represent this, I entreat you, to our mother; the harm is not yet great; it can easily be remediated when Ursule is sent back, whom Madame Parangon asks for with renewed insistence.

It is like a competition here to see who can make me more best wishes; I receive them equally from my master, as from his respectable spouse: but the caresses of the first are deceptive, and I distrust them: the terms they use have a double meaning for me... But in the end, I find myself in a state that one could call happy, if I did not suffer some reversals... They will stop soon enough, and when I no longer have the marks of my shame before my eyes,... I will be happier than I might expect.

Mademoiselle Manon has left home for six months; she is in a community whose [Mother] Superior is a relative; her mother and sister have accompanied her there. Would that our parents might write them a honest letter, simply showing them their esteem, without speaking of marriage in any way, and let Ursule be responsible for delivering it; as she should arrive no later than Sunday. I am counting on you for all that, my dear older brother; urging you to believe me, being filled with the most vivid affection for you and for all our brothers and sisters.

P.S. You will find in the included sheet of paper, the history of Mademoiselle Manon's seduction; and I believe that after you have read it, this unfortunate Demoiselle will appear a bit more excusable to you. She had written it to give to me instead of another paper that her cousin M. Gaudet had dictated to her, and which she remitted to me on the day that everything was discovered.

> *My dear husband: until the age of sixteen, I had hardly ever noticed that there were beings of an opposite sex from mine. My cousin Gaudet was the only person I liked; but I was still too young when he departed from the city; and you know that when he returned, I no longer had any choice in the matter. Having arrived at this period in my life when passions form, I fell into a disquietude and disgust for ordinary amusements which made me find them insupportable. I did not know to what to attribute this languorous state of the soul. The best I could conclude from my observations was this, that when I found myself in situations where there*

*were a large number of young men, my torment was as if suspended. But no one young man in particular attracted me; they all interested me equally; to the effect that it was less such and such a man whose presence gave me pleasure than an instinct that drew me towards men in general. (I was still in this state when I saw you in V***; it was I who gave you the small tap on the cheek, moved by I do not know what desire to engage you to cast your eyes on me.) The young men of the city of A*** are perhaps the least attractive in the world: coarse, vain, impertinent, indiscreet, sensual, overly fond of food and drink; what one needs, in order to put up with them, is to have very strong physical needs, and to have never seen anyone better. This was the case in which I found myself. However, I did not imagine myself with any of them, and my heart vacillated for an entire year.*

It was at this fatal juncture when my cousin Parangon was obliged to go to Paris. She proposed to me that I manage her household. My innocence was the cause of my presumption; I did not fear the danger because it was as yet unknown to me.

So I filled my cousin's shoes. Her hus-

band, without being too seductive, was however very dangerous for a young person of my character. He was about thirty-six years old: it is the age of maturity; he is witty, knows the ways of the world, has an unbridled taste for women, and a morality that aligns marvelously with all sorts of disorder. Such is the man into whose hands fell a girl lacking in experience, a girl pretty enough to merit someone's attempt to ruin her, and who bore in the donjon of her heart a secret enemy, ready to cede the place to the first assailant.

Several weeks passed [without incident] so as to give me a sense of the greatest possible security, supposing I had any distrust; but I did not have any, and I regarded the counsels that my cousin had given to me before her departure as the chimerical fears of a young woman who in the eyes of the world passed for an out-and-out prude; besides, her age, which was greater than mine by merely one year, did not inspire in me much deference to her counsels. Alas! I was ignorant at that time of the difference that a strong personality and a predilection for virtue makes between people who are equal in appearance.

At the end of about one month and a half, M. Parangon became more assiduous with me; his discourses were obliging, and sometimes flattering; he sought to stoke the fire that simmered in my bosom, by voluptuous readings; he had me read The Philosophical Tomb,[25] The Sopha,[26] *and several novels by Madame de Villedieu, wherein one sees married women listening to, and favoring, lovers; finally, he seduced both my mind and my heart simultaneously. But that was still not enough to triumph over my virtue and overcome the prejudices of a good education: to destroy them both, he procured impious books for me: the first was* The P . by M. de V***,[27] *which had only just come out. One could not have prescribed a more agreeable poison to consume: that work, which is without a doubt a masterpiece in its genre, at first captivated my mind by its charming lines, and finished by inspiring in me a contempt for the holy truths of Religion. In support of that*

---

[25]*The Philosophical Tomb: Le Tombeau Philosophique: or the Story of the Marquis de *** to Madame de ****, attributed to Jean-François de Bastide (AD 1724-1798).

[26]*The Sopha: Le Sopha, conte moral,* by Claude-Prosper Jolyot de Crébillon (AD 1707-1777).

[27]*La P.* de M. de V*** : *The P.* by M. de V***. Unattributable.

dangerous book came Christianity Unveiled; The Count de Boulainvilliers' Supper; The Holy Contagion; The Attempt on Prejudices; Bolingbroke; The Letters about Miracles; The Theists' Confession of Faith; *and several other works of the same stamp. But at the same time that M. Parangon was enlightening me, as he put it, he thought to introduce a corruption into my heart, which made me desire that what I was finding in those damnable books was the truth. Consequently, he gave me to read everything that lubricity dictated of the most infamous sort. I had never heard speak of immoral books; I accepted without question everything that he gave me, and I read them at first out of curiosity, soon out of pleasure; finally, I was asking for them.*

It was then that M. Parangon thought he could hazard several discourses. I received him as he deserved; the corruption of my heart was nothing but theoretical, so to speak, for the moment, and I was as reserved in practice as before. But it is quite well known that a virtue that has no more foundation cannot endure; imperceptibly I grew accustomed to hearing him say things that were much more restrained than my readings; and since one of my senses had lost its chastity, which was already no longer residing in my heart, the dangerous Enemy of my virtue thought that it could attack the others with impunity. I would hope that this information could be useful for young people to know, and if it were practicable, under an alias, to go public with it, I would do so with great zeal. As soon as he saw that I was listening to his discourses, he proceeded to act. His attempts at first were no more than a sort of somewhat loose banter; but imperceptibly he took greater liberties, with a view to stoking my sensibilities and making them revolt against a wavering virtue. He added a flattering language to that conduct, capable simultaneously of tickling my vanity and of instilling in me a compassion for the suffering that my incomparable *charms caused.*

It was nearly impossible for a girl of my age, of my temperament, and of my figure, to resist such a well-orchestrated attack. But I put up a good resistance for a period of time; then I ceded little by little; one liberty at first, then another, until the more decisive ones; I held the line there for a long while; my heart was corrupted by now; I was desirous of crossing the last barrier; but the sense of danger held me back; all too well did I know what could result from a more intimate commerce than what he had already had with me, and the idea of an accident made me shudder. Insofar as I did not mention this reason to him, he kept pressing me, but with some consideration for what he called my scruples; but as soon as I let out the word, and let him know the reason that was holding me back, it was all over for me. It is quite possibly the greatest imprudence that a girl could make, to position herself behind this feeble entrenchment. In fact, as soon as he knew the cause of my refusals, and that virtue had nothing to do with it, he was quick to speak to me about the means to avoid what I feared most; he spoke to me about several other women, and I had the misfortune, or rather the indignity, of yielding; for I do not pretend to attenuate my fault, by saying that he employed violence, although there is some truth to that, because eventually I consented.

But soon I noticed that the criminal precautions were often forgotten; I trembled; I flat out refused to lend myself to what was wanted of me. It was under these circumstances that a young apprentice came to live under my seducer's roof, someone whose *lovable simplicity furnished a new means of triumph to the man whom my refusals made despair. This young man was the same person who caught my eye in V*** and who has interested me ever since. My seducer had been pressed to ask for that young man from his parents, doubtless with a view to making him serve his designs on me; he was moreover accustomed to like maneuvers. As soon as that young man was living in his house, he waged another attack; he spoke to me about certain men who married their mistresses off to naïve young men, whom they favored. He praised village folk to me, and the talent they had of making their way in the world, provided they could find someone in a position to help them overcome their initial obstacles, etc. He had no difficulty persuading me once he had made me see on whom he had set his sights. He urged me to support him; judge for yourself with what pleasure I must have done so.*

So long as I had, for my seducer's pupil, the simple enjoyment merely that his beauty inspired in me, I shamelessly continued in my unprincipled affair, and I had the baseness to regard him as the dupe who was going to cover for my dishonor. But soon he assumed the tone and the attitude that so easily subjugates us, us women; his interesting and noble appearance assumed all the graces that he had been lacking for lack of experience; and my liking for him turned into feelings. It was then that virtue began to re-enter my heart coupled with true love. I no longer suffered my seducer except with repugnance, disgust, and soon horror. I could not yet free myself from him, however: how punished I was! And what a torture it is, that of loving someone passionately, and being forced to yield [to another]!... No, I do not believe that there is anything crueler in life. It was under these circumstances that the situation I feared most transpired. I took advantage of the situation to forbid my seducer from taking familiarities, and I sought all imaginable opportunities to lead my lover to take these same familiarities with me. I failed, and I was desperate as a result. My seducer suffered for it. Seeing as he could no longer hope I might grow tranquil, he worked night and day to conclude the marriage that he was planning.

The more I saw of my lover, the more I grew attached to him; from the inner recesses of my heart, I swore that I would love him, and him alone; it is

*what prevented me from dying of
shame for the deception I was about to
cause him; I proposed to myself that I
would repair the wrong so thoroughly,
by making him happy after our marriage, that my fault was a stroke of
good luck for him... Alas! that so flattering hope is lost forever! or rather...*

She stopped there, dear older brother; you can
see by this account, as sincere as if she had made it to
her Confessor, that it was practically impossible for
the poor Demoiselle not to have been deceived: it is
M. Parangon who is the wretched tempter, and who
will answer one day before God for all the harm he
has caused us, Mademoiselle Manon and me.

XXXVI.

November 20.

EDMOND TO FATHER D'ARRAS.

He speaks openly here.

If *everything has succeeded*, dear Father, it is to you
and M. Gaudet that I am indebted; your wise counsels
have saved my spouse and me, without causing me to
fall out with my parents, nor with my friends, among
whom Madame Parangon will always hold the first
rank. My father just wrote the letter that you were
asking for: my sister is with Madame Parangon; they
are inseparable, and their mutual attachment aug-
ments the happiness that I enjoy through your efforts.

I think like you, that it is on the dear Ursule that I must count in order to make peace with everyone. Absolutely nobody suspects our marriage: we will reveal it when everything is ready. But what I cannot stop admiring is how these circumstances have come together! Everything was made ready, everything was signed; M. Gaudet hastened the departure of my parents, he disconcerted them to the point that M. Parangon himself thought that he was crazy; he threw the contract and registers aside, made all that disappear without affectation: how easy it is to deceive candor, correctness, and simplicity! how that noble confidence humbled me, and how it freed me from remorse! We went to church; it was one o'clock; nobody but us witnesses; we could parody the saying of Denis: "See how the Gods favor the machinations of Swindlers!" – when I think on all that, I cannot help seeing in it a destiny that I could not avoid. Ah! What could I do? Manon would have killed herself otherwise, there can be no doubt about it; I saw the poison; and as you and M. Gaudet had very accurately pointed out, I would have been the cause of that calamity. In the end, she is my wife: it is a secret to keep for several years perhaps; but much more difficult to hide from my first friend, my brother; but I must. I thank you for the goodness you have shown in accepting the direction of consciences at the monastery where the mother and two sisters withdrew to: it is a consolation to me, in the separation that I was willing to condemn myself to, to know that you are often on hand there to speak with my spouse. Adieu, dear Father; serve us both by serving her.

XXXVII.

Pierrot to Edmond.

Difficult advice to follow.

It is decided, Edmond; my marriage to Marie-Jeanne will happen in one month from now; mark it on your calendar, with the intent of attending it with Ursule; and if Madame Parangon wanted to do us the honor, as well as Mademoiselle Tiennete, our father, our mother, my betrothed and I we would be overjoyed; and, to that effect, herewith is a letter from our dear father; on your side, do not forget in any way to engage them to do so. I am sure about the woman I am to marry, my Edmond; she is not like the girls of the city, who kiss the cheeks of one man, and give their hand to be kissed by another, as I have seen on a print at a Canon's in Au***. And look at you, free again; you should consider yourself too young for marriage; wait until you know your state in life, and leave it to M. Parangon's wife the trouble of finding you a wife; for it will be less dangerous to receive one from her hand than from your master's. Oh! the crafty gentleman! how he charmed us with his beautiful discourses and his benign attitude! Our father and our mother could not stop talking about him, when it was just us three together. Your Demoiselle Manon has made a good decision; for it appears that she is going to become a Religious. And you, my friend, take care to behave yourself; be a good fellow; listen to Madame Parangon and Mademoiselle Tiennete; their conversation is fine and good; they are nothing but wisdom and prudence, and I trust them to be good for you. But be careful not to look into their eyes: by golly! if what our brothers say is true, – how enticing they are! They will betray you, without their even knowing it. It is just the same with Marie-Jeanne; when it happens sometimes that she does not act completely to my liking, if I want to scold her, I need to lower my eyes; for if I look at her in the eyes, I become like a wet noodle: she has such a sweet look on her face, such a good little wink! and before you know it I don't know where I am anymore, and I say flat out what I should not say. Watch over Ursule: one watches out for others better than for oneself; doing so, keep an eye on all her activities. I do not have anything else to say, dear brother, other than that I am very busy, and that, although I would like to, I am unable to write long letters. I embrace Ursule; Marie-Jeanne sends her greeting to the both of you, and our other brothers and sisters do the same.

LETTER FROM M. R***[28] TO MADAME PARANGON.

Madame,

I take the liberty of writing to you, with the purpose of thanking you for all the kindness you have shown to my children, for which I will hold a very perfect gratitude for the remainder of my life. For you are with respect to my daughter, Madame, what Naomi was for Ruth; and with respect to my son, what Michal, the daughter of King Saul, was for David, who helped him

---

[28]M. R***: Edmond's father.

descend from a window into a basket, in order to escape his enemies: this is why, Madame, I entrust to your care, and to your protection, both brother and sister, like the holy man Tobias entrusted his son to the Angel who was supposed to lead him to Raguel, where he kept him safe from the ambushes of the Demon and had him marry a virtuous wife; urging you to be towards them as Deborah was with respect to Barak, whom she encouraged, and to act as the salvation against their enemies, as Jael did to Sisera, general of the army of Jabin, the King of Moab, who planted a tent spike in his temple, and like the generous Judith did to the impious Holofernes: imploring you in addition, Madame, if they should have the ill fortune of falling into some error, to encourage them to remember themselves, and to repatriate themselves with their superiors, as the woman from Tekoah did who, by an ingenious similitude, reconciled Absalom to his father David, sent as she had been by Joab. I know, Madame, that you have all the virtues of Sarah and the graces of Rachel, who so pleased her husband Jacob that he served Laban fourteen years on account of her. The only thing you lack is to be favored by the Lord like Anna, who prayed before the parvis of the Tabernacle in Shiloh, when the High Priest Eli thought her drunk, and asked her what she had, and then predicted to her that she would have a son, who was the holy Prophet Samuel. I wish you the same benediction, Madame, urging you to accept the prayer that I dare make to you, to honor us with your presence at the wedding of my oldest son, whom by the grace of God we are going to marry soon. Grant us this favor, Madame, and believe me that your honorable attendance will double our joy. It is a good and honest girl whom my son Pierre marries; she has a comely and friendly face, with an even more gracious temperament, such as I imagine Rebecca had when Eliezer led her to marry the young Isaac, son of the patriarch Abraham his master. As for yourself, Madame, we will look on you here as the most beautiful floret in the crown of flowers that the bride wears, and just like the Shunammite in the Song of Songs, which the wise King Solomon sang. My wife pays you her very sincere respects, entreating you to fulfill our supplication. And coming to a close now, I have the honor of being, with a perfectly respectful gratitude for your precious kindness,

MADAME, your very humble and very obedient servant,

*– E. R***.*

The marriage will be held January 13.

Written in Sacy, this December 20, 1749.

XXXVIII.

1750.

EDMOND TO HIS FATHER AND MOTHER.

Letter of Happy New Year and hypocrisy.

My very dear and very honored Father, and my very dear and very honored Mother,

I acquit myself, at the start of this year, of a duty that is extremely agreeable to me to fulfill, as it involves wishing you a happiness that devolves on us all. May you, very dear father and very dear mother, pass every day of the coming year as joyously as you do now, as I am writing this to you! And may your satisfaction result especially from the conduct of your children, and above all my conduct, as well as that of the dear Ursule who joins me! However, dear father and dear mother, it happens sometimes that children, carried away by circumstances, commit faults that their heart and their will have no part in. I hope that if I have committed any, or if I commit any, you will have some indulgence towards me, your son. I have acquitted myself, these Christmas holidays, of the duties of our holy Religion, in order to prepare myself for the start of this new year; Father d'Arras has heard me. My sister has done similarly, and surely more dignantly than me, who always commits some faults which I am quite contrite for, but which it is out of my control to avoid. I place my hope in your kindness and, if I should ever have need of things of consequence, that your hearts will always be open to your Edmond.

There are cases, dear father and dear mother, when one feels the full extent of the duty of being a child more than ever; it is when one has entered into, or is on the verge of entering into, the bonds of marriage, as my dear older brother does; one imagines at such times what those who gave us life might desire for us; and according to this desire, one makes the same homage to those Authors of our days. I do not say this without purpose, and I hope one day to unbare to you what is in my heart.

Everyone here whom I have spoken to about you, dear father and dear mother, send you their best wishes; among the principal people, I will name M. and Madame Parangon, Madame Palestine and her two daughters, and above all Mademoiselle Manon, who is attached to you like a daughter, and who is flattered by a reciprocal feeling from you; M. Loiseau and Mademoiselle Tiennete as well pay you their respects.

I have the honor of being with the most profound veneration, etc.

FROM URSULE.

I am adding to what my brother has written, very dear father and very dear mother, to wish you Heaven's blessings and to ask you for yours. My submission, my respect, my unbounded feelings, that is all that I can offer to you; my brother is happier; he sends to you the things that he knows that you love; but whatever the tokens of affection that he sends, I am sure that they are far below what we both feel for you.

I am with a profound respect and a filial devotion, dear papa, etc.

XXXIX.

EDMOND TO GAUDET.

His corruption begins to manifest itself, although he still displays feelings and a good heart; but since the marriage he entered into, and which he lacked delicacy by so doing, he proceeds with large strides down the road to vice. My children, it is not without reason that what our scatterbrained people of today call prejudices were made sacred formerly; they are the safeguards of our mores, and whoever respects them erects a wall between crime and himself.

I write to you now from my paternal home, dear friend; pleasures surround me, and I abandon myself to them without constraint. My faith, you are right, one must enjoy oneself; it is not lacking in Religion to employ the gifts that God has given to us: this maxim, to be honest, can lead far; but, my dear Mentor, to this admirable art that you have for dispelling scruples, you join a consummate prudence; so I abandon myself to it, and I consider your acquaintance to be the greatest kindness that Father d'Arras, our good friend, has done for me; and my union with your lovely cousin as the greatest benefit that he has procured for me. Without you, I would have had the stupidity of not moving forward on a marriage that makes me the master of twenty-five thousand ecus... Apropos of which, is it really true that the mother and older sister are going to take the veil so that I do not repent the sacrifice I make for them? If they fear to incommode me, they are wrong; I am not a hard man; I love those who love me; it is up to them to decide; and when Manon will have gotten rid of her burden, I think that I will not love her less, but as if it had never happened. Your principles are excellent, dear Mentor, I savor them more than ever; all that [morality] is merely ideas and prejudices. You have made me acquainted with tons of women in the same situation as mine, and whose husbands however are so tranquil! so many girls whose lovers believe them to be Lucreces! so many virtues that are lost and which are reborn every day from their ashes! That, in fact, I should be thoroughly consoled by my small ordeal. It is to you, dear Mentor, that I owe all my tranquility... But you do know just how wicked you are! My wife would not be obliged to you for the counsel you give me: but your thoughts on the punishment of *lex tal-*

ionis[29] are really quite nice... Would I be wrong to imagine you a friend of the great Sleeper? (It is a name that we give him between ourselves because he does not open his curtains until eleven o'clock.) I tell you this, and you respond to me: What harm is there? A man born for himself, who sacrifices everything to himself, who wants everything made to serve his pleasures... My faith! that's him, trait for trait; I believe I can understand M. Parangon; his wife is here; she did not want to quit Ursule's side; and Tiennete is with them as well. You do know, despite your jokes, which I find inappropriate in this case, that my lovely mistress makes me believe in the virtue of women! What were you wishing to say, the other day, with your suppressed laughter, when I was speaking to you about her attachment to Ursule? I confess that I did not understand you. But, whatever the case, the respect that I feel for Madame Parangon is a pleasure for me; I feel no more pleasure loving Manon than I do respecting the virtuous Colète C***.

I will not deny, my friend, that the celebration, and the joy that animates it, have made an impression on my senses. And can you guess what the first object was that love chose to stir them with? A seductive beauty; a modest, naïve, and pure young person, crowned with flowers; my sister-in-law finally; not that I desired for a single moment to obtain something from her who gives herself to my brother (the very thought of it fills me with horror!); but she pleased me; and I thoroughly enjoyed dancing with her, chatting with her. I did not kiss her but once, because I

___

[29]*lex talionis*: the law of an "eye for an eye..."; in other words, a punishment equal to the crime.

felt that I did it with too much emotion. Do not go repeating all my follies to my wife: besides, this feeling did not last. A young lady from the area that my mother hails from (whom I was not indifferent to in the past), who was invited with the rest of her family, although she is a distant relation on my mother's side, arrived very late. The groom received her and had me do the honors. I acquitted myself as towards an ancient Inclination. The little cousin is charming; her waist is svelte; her eyes are more tender than bright; her mouth is small and fresh; her whole face is smiling and naïve; her breasts are half-formed; her legs, my God, are the most exquisite legs I have ever laid my eyes on. She just turned sixteen years old. Her complexion is not at all rosy, but it has a charming suggestion which seems to be waiting for pleasure and love to arrive in order to put some color into it. That is exactly what I will try to do, my good and faithful Mentor. My faith, it would have been desirable for Telemachus that his had resembled you; Mademoiselle Eucharis would have been all the better served for it, but not Antiope! I really need to be careful here, however: you can sense what I have to deal with: my parents, my older brother especially, before whom I will need to disguise myself for a long time now; and above all that, Madame Parangon; it is she whose esteem I fear losing the most. Everything goes rather well however, thanks to the innocence of my young conquest, and to what remains of an old trust, otherwise quite well merited in every sense. At the first opportunity, I will more fully inform you. Adieu, my papa.

XL.

THE SAME TO THE SAME.

This letter is one that I would have removed if it was not needed to show the progression of vice. He recounts herein how he seduced our cousin.

It is all set with the little cousin, my dear Mentor; what a pleasure these village girls are! They are made of such a charming naïvety; and then you deflower them. That's how the world works, as you once said; whoever loses one, finds two. Quite foolish anyone who is afflicted by it! Whoever takes up with the young person, will he not be in the same situation that the great Sleeper got me into? *A good cat, a good rat; each man for himself; I will take them where I find them.* I could pile on here as many proverbs as Sancho Panza, each one more consoling than the last. A good friend is a treasure, and you prove it to me: we will do penance for our mischief when we are old, isn't that right, my friend?

My little cousin gave in to me with an inexpressible grace, as you are about to hear. Yesterday evening, when everyone had retired, and when my dear brother got drunk, or ought to have gotten drunk, on licit pleasures, fully occupied as he was with making his chaste and pretty better half lose the name of maiden, I was looking for forbidden ones as I led the little Laure into her private room. I left the room to let her get into bed, after having urged her not to extinguish the candle because I did not have another. She made haste so as not to keep me waiting; and when, *between two sheets, she arranged her charms*, she called me, – "Cousin, I'm in bed; come and find your light..." – I immediately entered the room again; I let the candle fall and stepped on the wick as if by mistake; I pretended to be very upset by this accident; finally, I approached the delightful girl's bed to wish her good night and to embraced. One kiss, two kisses...; the little cousin was smiling: a liberty; the little cousin defended herself, but so clumsily! And, in order to cover her breasts, she left all the rest exposed. Imagine for yourself what would become of me if anyone only so much as suspected a similar undertaking!... Today, the little person appeared distracted to me, lost in thought: the lesson she received yesterday occupies her mind obviously, she deserves to be visited again, and I hope to repeat it this evening. And here she is now: I leave you for a moment: friendship is never so pressed for time as love is...

I must tell you the sequel to my adventure. Laure timidly came up to me; she dared not lift her gaze. – "What's wrong, Laurote?"[30] I said, "You seem sad to me." – "Oh! no, it's just that I'm shy." – "My goodness, shy! a pretty girl like you, must she always be shy? Come closer, my little cousin." – "O, nay, nay." – "How's that! 'nay'? Have you changed your mind about me already?" – "No, my cousin; but don't you have to marry me now?" – "Don't worry about that!" – "The honest truth?" – "And why not? Are you not lovable? Are we not a pair?" – "If you promise me..." – "I swear it to you." (I'm not such a bad rascal, as you can see. Eh! What do you think? I do have remorse though: this sort of life does not exactly

---

[30]Original footnote: In the countryside, one says *Laurote* instead of *Laure* or *Laurette*.

conduce to the straight and narrow.) – "Can I believe you then?" – "Ah! my dear Laurote! Would you take me for a miserable liar then?" – "I didn't say that." – "Have I given you any reason for these unjust suspicions!" – "Nay, nay, my cousin; and I recall that we loved each other dearly in our youth." – "Then you don't consider me capable of lying to you?" – "Oh, my God, no!" – "Will you prove it to me then, that you really believe me?" – "I will prove it to you whenever you like." – I took her at her word; she defended herself: I pretended to be disheartened; perfidious tears fell from my eyes; I said that she did not love me. The delightful child bent over backwards to assure me that she did: finally she became gentle like a poor little lamb;[31] and it is at that moment that I can flatter myself for having ensnared her. I am not at all resolved to leave her like that; this little treasure infinitely attracts me; in all honesty, the pleasure that she inspires in me is so ardent that if it continues... We will see how it all turns out. What if I were to grow infatuated with her? She goes home in three days; I would have a reason to repent my wickedness; for, once my brother's nuptials are over, when and how would I see her again?... It is a secret, my friend: it is a confession that I make to you, as I were making it to Father d'Arras; you do understand me, yes?

XLI.

THE SAME TO THE SAME.

---

[31]Original footnote: It might not be a bad thing for young people to read these lines, things that happen so frequently in society.

A mix of good and evil; but the latter takes the upper hand.

One week without writing to me! Are you ill, dead, buried, interred? or is it perhaps the little cousin...[32] My faith, all the above, my papa: the little cousin has very nearly consumed all my strength. I love her, I adore her, I am mad about her, I cannot leave her: I have kept her until this very moment. What might seem singular to you is that now that my liking for her shows, the virtuous Madame Parangon has made it her duty to protect it; one could say that every object is good [to her], provided it keeps me from her cousin. But in the end, I lose all my pleasures today; Laurette departs; but we ourselves will stay here for another week; Madame Parangon desires it.

So nothing was able to cool my mother-in-law and sister-in-law's zeal! *They have both taken the veil.* And sounding my heart, I find that I am upset by it! If I suspected that you or d'Arras had a hand in this, I would be upset with you... as one can be upset with friends who are too fervent. *My wife gets along well:* this news has given me immeasurable pleasure. Just between you and me, my papa, I propose to be unfaithful only until our reunion: afterwards, we will live together like two turtledoves, always yearning for each other's tenderness, always satisfying each other's desires. Consequently, you see that it is unnecessary to embark me on the adventure that you mentioned; if I was determined to have my little cousin

---

[32]Original footnote: The words in italics are from a letter by Gaudet to Edmond, which is lost, for the reasons mentioned in the Letter LV. In these cases, what is repeated in the response is always found in italics, as it is here. (Editor's note)

furtively show up in the city, would she not be discovered? What chaos that would cause in the family! No, that cannot happen. Besides, my wife is worth it; she loves me, and I love her in return, if only by gratitude. I am all for moral virtues; without them, life is not worth living, for one ought to redeem one's vices by something. You think, and you do better than you do not say, my papa; you have humanity; you are the most obliging, generous man; you act secretly for the good of strangers; and you would have me do an injustice to my wife!... Ah! allow me to imitate your virtues given I have assumed your vices... Besides, you have perhaps a *retentum*, which I don't quite understand.

I am not against my mother-in-law having given me *all her fortune in hard cash*, and that you *work on my behalf to acquire that lovely property near the convent of the Benedictines*. The meadows, the adjoining lands, the bran and flour mills, the surrounding vineyards and orchards can produce, according to what I have been told, three thousand six hundred livres; it's more than the interest of our total; I subscribe to it, and you can close the deal at *seventy thousand francs, with a good bribe*, given that *Madame Palestine* says she has *another seventy-five thousand at the notary's*. When I think about all that this good Lady does for me, I cannot help accusing myself of ingratitude; I am sorely lacking with respect to her daughter, in consideration of whom she cedes all her fortune to me; M. Parangon did more harm to us, to my spouse and me, than anyone can imagine![33]

---

[33]Original footnote: here we see a flash of understanding that penetrates Edmond's heart. He often has similar ones; but they

I am upset with all those who informed me: why did they do it! Without them, I would have respected myself more... Yes, my wife is an imprudent woman; Madame Parangon... oh! as far as she is concerned, whatever she does, I do not know why, but it always seems well founded: but I am upset with Mademoiselle Tiennete, with M. Loiseau; I endeavor to be upset with my sister even... however, where is Ursule's mistake? I am in a bad mood; let us invoke more happy thoughts.

You make me envisage for the future a very agreeable life; I see a sketch of it in advance. We will be united; we will see each other every day; I hope that one day we can reconcile Madame Parangon with my wife; then we will be a charming little society, and you will be the philosopher of it, and d'Arras the director. I so desire that arrangement, and from now on I will work to prepare for it. Madame Parangon has always been so friendly towards me that I have high hopes for a soul as beautiful as hers is... I will accompany the little cousin home. Adieu, my Mentor: moderate your pleasures, and take care of your health for those who love you.

XLII.

The Same to the Same.

Here is yet another peril.

Imagine, my dear Mentor, a vessel floating on a stormy sea, sometimes it makes headway, and some-

---

are glimmers that shed light on his turpitude without correcting it.

times it is thrown in the opposite direction to which it tends; now imagine my heart these last four days, ever since that little cousin of mine has departed. The attention that I had paid her has, so to speak, clouded my eyes to the attractions of other women; hers however were not the most dangerous!... Since the tumult has ended, and all the strangers have departed, and now that we are calm again in our little family circle, we take advantage of some of the beautiful moments that the season accords us, in order to promenade within the grounds of the paternal house, my mistress, Tiennete, M. Loiseau, Ursule, Marie-Jeanne, and I. Tiennete and Loiseau go off on their own; Ursule most often speaks with the new bride; and I am with Madame Parangon; I assist her to walk, and I believe I see a certain satisfaction in her eyes. For me, the moment when she leans on my arm a little, my heart begins pumping; I would like to support the entire weight of that precious body.

Our conversation yesterday focused on Laurette; Madame Parangon asked me what I thought of that lovely girl. I thought that I needed to be careful: "She's nice," I said. – "Nice? You are reserved in your praises." – "But, yes, she is quite nice." – "As for myself, Monsieur, I think she is charming." – "And I would agree with you." – "I find an air of seductive youth about her." – "That is true." – "That young person deserves much." – "Yes, Madame." – "But much more I suppose than the coolness of your responses, Monsieur." – "I put all the warmth that I can into them, Madame... In fact, *I agree with you; it is true; yes, Madame*." – "That is warmer... I am wrong, and I was mistaken!" – "Let us suppose,

Madame, that my responses had the coolness that you find in them; is it my fault?" – "The fault is mine, you will see." – "One could do worse; I know an object that erases everything that pretends to shine beside it; what can those who are insufficient do?" – "I don't understand, Edmond." – "I do not doubt it; Madame, what I am saying is doubly unintelligible to you." – "Eh! what makes you say that?" – "The fact of the matter, Madame, is that I was desirous of you ordering me to make it more clear to you." – At this moment, she twisted her foot; she took a wrong step: I kept her from falling by holding her in my arms; what I felt is beyond pleasure; I could not resolve to put her back down on the ground. A look (I believe that purity itself had cast it), a simple look imposed on me; I timidly asked her to sit down. She did, because she was feeling some pain. I let her see how much I feared that it did not develop into something serious: a lovely smile reassured me. I touched her foot; I moved it; (ah! friend, in all my life I have never experienced anything quite like it!) and I saw in her eyes an embarrassment that had nothing severe about it. We picked up our conversation again.

"You would like to make me understand" (it was she who was speaking) "that Laure pleased you but only moderately? I had gotten the impression that you were strongly taken by her." – "There is in my heart, Madame, an obstacle to the attachment you speak of." – "So much the worse! I was interested in Laure." – "You would also be interested in this other..." – She brusquely interrupted me, saying "I do not know why I started up this conversation again; it bores me." – "Then let us drop it, Madame, and allow me to speak about you." – "About me? Eh! what could we say?" – "That you are worthy of the deepest respect as well as the most tender feelings, and that that is what you inspire in me." – "I reciprocate these feelings, by a sincere friendship; I share it between you and your sister; to the effect that each of you possesses it in its entirety." – I dared to kiss her hand. She quickly pulled it away from me, saying, "This sort of thing does not please me, except from Ursule." – "Everything is not equal then, and already we encounter the difference?" – "The equality is only in my heart." – "How will I recognize it, if the signs are not the same? You are going to make me jealous." – "You would rather I be unjust?" – "No, Madame; I shall always fear that a precious good, that nothing will assure me the possession of, might be taken away from me." – "Nobody can take it away from you." – "You prefer my sister?" – "But, you are becoming demanding, Monsieur? I want to be free in the distribution of my gifts." – "You are cross because I kissed your hand." – "But, Edmond, what is the nature of the feelings that you have for me?" – "Ah! Madame! They are such as you inspire them to be: tender and respectful; your kindnesses and your attractions; I do not distinguish between them." – "Let's leave it at that: this is not at all an ordinary flirting; I know my duties: let's be brother and sister together; assume the feelings that are suitable to that quality, just as I have assumed them; Edmond, I love you, and you will know soon enough in just what way; I am flattered to be able to make your happiness by sure means; but I wait for you to discover them, and for your soul to be more anchored. Eh! May it please God that I can, better than another person, fix the irresolution that I discover in you." – "Irresolution! I no longer have any, Madame..." – My sisters and Tiennete, having approached us at this time, Madame Parangon interrupted our conversation in order to respond to something they said; then she got up; she walked, limping a little. I was practically charmed by this little accident, and you know why: she was obliged to lean on my arm. We returned to the house.

In the house, another amusing scene, dear Mentor. Madame Parangon and my sister retired to their room. Above it is a tiny cubicle where I knew there to be a small opening: in the most adroit manner possible, I very carefully slid up to it. I did not catch the first words of the conversation, but here is how the beautiful Lady responded: "No, my daughter, I will never forget that I am married; my Husband's deviations would not authorize my own, I know it too well: but I want your brother to be happy, I can see to it, and it is the only pleasure that is permitted me... I don't know, but I sense the inquietudes... I would like him to dare to love me: I am quite sure to restrain him within the just bounds; a managed love does not corrupt mores in any way; his are still pure"; (oh! Gaudet, how this expression made a sad impression on me!); "if he loved me, I would separate him from Manon, from that girl who is unworthy of him, who is capable of vilifying him, and who wanted to deceive him; it would not be difficult then, when age would make him more mature, to lead him to the object that I propose for him. Unable to hope, not daring even to nourish the hope that he could be mine, it is to my sister that I destine him; I have never seriously thought about Laurette, nor the young Edmée; I would have only wanted that those young people might have led him away from a seductress, because my sister is still only a child; you know her, she is ten years old; her features, as they develop, become more flattering with each passing day; Edmond would be my joy, I believe he would be hers. He would be my brother; by that title, I could love him in an innocent way; I would no longer blush to follow a penchant full of sweetness... Ursule! ah if you only knew! jealousy is a cruel torment!... Earlier, he took my hand, he kissed it... it required all my reasoning to pull away; I had to grow upset, to desensitize myself to a criminal satisfaction... Then, as he spoke to me, my imagination, in spite of myself, painted for me the pleasure I would have had doing the same to him in turn... But I speak too much, and I forget that the whiff of a guilty love could tarnish the purity of my friendship with you." – "I find great pleasure in listening to you." – "Then I have been too distant, Ursule." – "No, it is because I love you, because I love my brother, and because you love him." – "This feeling, which is a virtue in your heart, is not [the same] in mine." – "... And in yours as well." – "No, my daughter; one more step and it could become a crime." – "You would never take that step." – "Eh! who can say! whoever looks for danger will perish... Ah! my dear Ursule!" – "My loving, my respectable friend! You are crying! Let, let me collect your tears!" – "Let us save Edmond from that passion that I fear; yes, even if it means that I must have no rest, we must absolutely do it." – "If my brother loves me, he will renounce it; I will tell him that I demand it of his friendship." – "Be careful, my friend! It is by love that one combats love; discourses, reasonings, friendship even, do nothing against this passion... I wish I could describe for you the state of my heart: when I saw your brother show interest in this young person who just left us, I felt joy; I said to myself, she will efface Manon; she is less dangerous than Manon; she is not deceitful, or vile, like Manon; just now, I have sounded him; the coolness that he gave me to believe he had for her, charmed me! what to make of it?" – "That you wish that he loves you and you alone." – Lifting her eyes to Heaven, she said "Ingenuousness has just spoken..." Then to my sister, she said, "And it is also what I fear, my child. Without your friendship, how unhappy I would be!" – "You have my heart in its entirety; yes, all of it." – "Ursule!... my dear girl!" – "My respectable friend!..." – "You love me a lot then?" – "Words fail me; but let my caresses prove it to you..."

Now the quill drops from my hands. Ah, God! how happy Ursule was!... Tiennete entered, and she joined them. Imagine for yourself this charming group of women; tell me if Cupid himself would not have preferred them to that of the Graces?... – "Ah! my good friends," Madame Parangon exclaimed, "how sweet these pleasures are! they leave no remorse; one fears neither infidelity, nor inconstancy! Such sweet things do not come from the mouths of perfidious people: charming girls, your hearts are as pure as you are beautiful!"

As it was the hour to sit down to table, Tiennete exited from the room in order to assist my mother and sisters. I went downstairs; but my emotion was so great that instead of going to be beside Madame Parangon, I took a walk in the garden. The supper was cheerful; as you might imagine, I had to participate. The eyes of every one of our good family were fixed on the beautiful Lady, and I enjoyed their admiration for her. My brothers contended for the honor of rendering her some service; my sisters could not help being a little jealous of Ursule; and that adorable woman, when she notices it, demonstrates to all of them how flattered she is by the value that they place on her affection. It is not her beauty alone that makes such a great impression on everyone; Ursule is perhaps just as cute; but Madame Parangon is... she is herself; as much to say, the epitome of beauty; another woman cannot have the graces, the inexpressible charm that moves hearts and subjugates them, but only insofar as she approximates her; I do not know whether that air of benevolence, that ease of manner that is all her own, if all that naturally came to her; or whether the Capital, as they say, lent them to her; but it does not matter: she has them nonetheless. Oh! I want to see it, that so vaunted Capital, where the women enchant, even those without beauty, and stir passions without being faithful, where they govern men without bothering to hide their despotic authority, and where they make even their most decided defects adored; I want to see it soon; I am burning with desire.[34]

On getting up from the table, I passed into Madame Parangon's room. Our conversation was inconsequential, because she asked me to read a new

---

[34]Original footnote: You will see it in short order, unfortunate man!

book which she had received earlier in the day. They are the letters of Héloïse to Abelard, in somewhat mediocre, or rather bad, French verse, to be perfectly frank. But how they moved us! I say "us" because... you understand the rest. Adieu, my friend. Do you not see that Madame Parangon has almost made me forget that I have a wife? Tell her that I am doing well, and tell her that I will write to her at the first opportunity to let her know of my return.

XLIII.

MADAME PALESTINE TO EDMOND.

Manon is injured and goes into labor.

The physician, M. Tiennot, will tell you, my dear son, about the accident that has happened to my daughter your spouse. Believe me when I say to you that if Heaven should take her from me, my resolutions towards you would not change. By this note, I contract the obligation to fulfill them. My oldest daughter sends you her greetings. The poor, ill woman embraces you with all her heart. Your sincere friend and good mother, – MARIE Q***, widow PALESTINE.

XLIV.

Same day.

EDMOND TO MANON.

How can someone express the same feelings for so many different objects of affection! The city is a dan-

*gerous place for someone who has a heart made like
Edmond's.*

Take courage, dear heart; the accident that just befell
you will not have any unfortunate consequences for
you; the physician assures me of it; if there were the
least danger, he would not have left your side, although he has left you in good hands; for you know,
as everyone in town knows, the merit of M. Berryat.
Take care of your health then for your husband, and
have not the least disquietude with respect to all the
rest. The night of eternal silence covers our dishonor,
which is no longer a dishonor since nobody knows
about it. It is now that I plan to surrender myself to all
the sweetness of being yours; nothing will distract me
from it; and I place all the hope of my future happiness on your sincere reciprocation.

I receive at the same time a letter from M.
Parangon, which I burned after having read it. He informs me that the child has been taken away from you
and baptized in a village at more than eight leagues
from here (it's Pourrain), under his father's name, and
that they have disguised the name of his mother in
this way: *Enitselap*; he is sure that it will live, despite
the manner in which it has seen the light of day; that
the very desire to have a child made him decide to seduce you; he assures me that, despairing of having a
child by his wife, he sought only to procure for himself, by another woman, the satisfaction of being a father; that, now that everything he had set out to do has
come to pass, he should have no more worries, provided I can assure him of being content with my fate.
He makes plans for the establishment of this child,

whom he will find the means to assure the fortune of; but you imagine how much all that still sounds like a pipe dream. It does not matter; I bring it up merely to amuse you, and to flatter your heart; for I do not have the injustice of finding it bad that you have a mother's womb now; I would despise you if you did not love, for the rest of your life, what you have carried in your womb.

What he then tells me about your cousin Gaudet, and about Father d'Arras, surprises me less than you might suppose. I know how free the first person's manner of thinking is; but everything that might be said, and everything that would have made me hate him when I was without experience, I now tolerate.[35] As for Father d'Arras, do we not already know how he is thought about in the Cloisters? My dear, we must take men as they are, and make friends with them. As for you, I declare that I will always depend on your virtue; if you deceived me, and I found out about it, contempt would be my vengeance: if, on the other hand, you are faithful to me, I will consider what is merely your duty as a grace, and I will have the same gratitude towards you. Your happiness, and mine, depend on our mutual affection; and when a wife is as lovely as you are, when she adds wit to beauty, it is her own fault if she does not find in her husband an honest man, a lover, a spouse, and a friend.

I do not grow tired of writing to you, but you

---

[35]Original footnote: This is what always happens when one puts oneself in the position of going easy on a blackguard through vile confidences.

will grow tired reading me. Adieu, sweetheart: I embrace your mother and your sister: tell them that I find them to be more than generous; and that if any misfortune had arisen, there would have been refusals on my part as sincere as the offers were on theirs. A thousand obliging things to the dear mother Prioress; she is a relative whom I will adore for my entire life.

Your friend, your lover, and your husband, etc.

XLV.

February 20.

MANON TO D'ARRAS.

No rest for the wicked.

And there you have him, just as you wanted him, it seems to me; what more could you desire? One person seeks to deceive him; the other to harden him; you to tranquilize him; and me, I am the suffering victim: this role displeases me; pass it on to M. Gaudet and to the other; it goes against my character: let them work something out. Ah, God! how annoying it is, how cruel, to have lost one's self-respect, that salutary restraint that keeps us in check more than religion and laws, forever powerless unless all their strength were put into it!... If I had had that self-respect, would my seducer have obtained yesterday's promise?... But one must practice virtue!... I will practice it; but if I am found out, let them tremble! *(Without signature.)*

XLVI.

February 22.

EDMOND TO M. LOISEAU.

*He makes known his marriage to Mademoiselle
Manon.*

You know the reason for my secret sorrows, dear friend; I have confessed to you what was humiliating to me, and what convinced me of all the baseness of the action that I took, by deceiving my parents. To lie on such an occasion! to keep a brother whom I love in the dark! to be false with a woman like Madame Parangon! to shut my heart to Ursule, to your friend, to you yourself! I could no longer resist: I have chosen you, for this painful confession, and I do not repent of it; the very love [that you have for me] could not make you indiscreet; but the burden of my confidence will not encumber you for long. We were interrupted at so inopportune a moment,[36] that I could not catch you up on my present dispositions; I will fill you in on what your departure prevented me from telling you.

My wife was in grave danger when I wrote to her; I knew it, but I dissimulated it; I am told that my letter gave her so much joy that a fortunate turn of events occurred, which took her from danger. I saved her life for a second time then; you know that the good we do for others endears us more than the bene-

---

[36]Original footnote: He had begun his confidence to him in S***.

fits we receive.[37] She has left the Convent: nothing transpired. On seeing her [again], I found her so pretty that I could not regret the sacrifice. And then, it is a delicious and new ragout for me, all these veils of mystery that we are obliged to wrap ourselves in. Since nobody knows all the interest that I take in her, in the circles that we frequent, I am told quite frankly what other people think about her: so far, everyone has only praise for her, each in his own manner. One person sighs for her, and tells me so; another person expresses himself cavalierly, and wishes me to do the same: Ellipud would like to spend one of his nights with her, even if it were his last; Des-F*** would sacrifice everything, including his impertinence, for her; the handsome Etiferreip, his mirror and his fatuity; Ch***, his woods and smallholdings; Bell**, his chateau; including but not limited to the automaton B*** de *** who would sell his fertile fields in Varzi for her. And yet, I am not at ease; I feel that a young person who lives alone with a girl who serves him, and whom he spends all his evenings with in obscurity, cannot endure for long in that situation without giving ample cause for gossip, ten times more venomous here than anywhere else, as you know. I see no way out except in an intimate liaison with Madame Parangon and the two others, whom you call so fittingly *the three Graces*; Manon would make the number complete: for you know that poets are shared in the afterlife, and that the ancients admit four as often as three; what is more, no matter what opinion you have, one can always be reconciled; Madame

---

[37]Original footnote: A fine truth, to which not enough attention is given: it is what makes us so sensitive to the injustice of ingrates.

Parangon will be Venus. I was saying then that a liaison[38] with *the three Graces* would remedy all our inconveniences, and it would preserve us from the ambushes of the great Sleeper, if he did not persevere in the feelings he displays. But how to arrive at that? One would need to reveal everything: my beautiful mistress is so generous that that is not what embarrasses me; but on seeking to find solace, I am sure to upset her most violently.

Let's talk about you for a moment, my friend: will you soon be returning to this town? Madame Parangon just told me that your friend's parents appear disposed to listen to reason. To give you their daughter's hand in marriage is the only position they could take. Mademoiselle Tiennete is just the opposite of Manon; possessing the most complete innocence, she has the upper hand on her. I would counsel you against choosing your small town, or Au***, as a place to settle down in; I would prefer, in your shoes, either the Capital or Dijon; I have my own reasons for this proposition; whatever city you chose would become my home, and I would set myself up near you; consequently, it is imperative that Manon and Mademoiselle Tiennete should become friends. I have already alerted my wife as to your betrothed's true status; she seemed very surprised to me, and urged me to work out a way for her to repair her wrongs with that lovely girl.

M. Gaudet, whom you appear to be strongly against, does not deserve all the bitterness of your re-

---

[38]liaison: as in a mutual understanding, but who can help the speaker from revealing more than he wishes to give away?

proaches; as for Father d'Arras, he is not suited to his station, I agree with you; but at least he is not a hypocrite; he has shown himself to be open with us. You seem to refuse to the former the quality even of being an honest man; and me, I accord him the following titles: a faithful, discrete, sincere friend; although too avid for certain pleasures (and so much the worse for the girls whose fathers and mothers are negligent, or for the husbands whose wives are easy!), he is otherwise incapable of procuring these pleasures for himself by base or vilifying means. Over the course of several days, he developed some principles that seemed so clear to me that I could not help but concede [to his line of reasoning]. Hurry up and return; we will chat with him about these interesting matters...[39] I will not finish my letter at this time. I hear a great deal of noise in the house; if the occasion is favorable, I will profit thereby to put into execution a plan that we are entertaining, my wife and I.

The following day.

I was quite agreeably interrupted in my letter to you yesterday: it was Madame Parangon's younger sister who had arrived. The *three Graces* received her with an equal tenderness of feeling. She is a real gem, this little Fanchette. Imagine for yourself the traits of this girl, her smile, with a cheerfulness that her older Sister seems to have lost. The shared joy appeared so well founded to me that I could not believe a better occasion could have presented itself than to broach

---

[39]Original footnote: One can see the clear principles in question here, in the Letter XCVII.

the visit that Manon wished to pay her cousin. I sounded out this latter person. At first, I saw surprise and anxiety paint itself on everyone's face. – "How do you know?" she said to me. "Are you her confidant? Did she choose you to present her? What does she want here?" – I responded: "Madame, your indulgence and your friendship: she deserves both; deign to hear her out, she has a thousand things to tell you; suffer her to pay you a visit as soon as today, immediately." – The *three Graces'* surprise augmented with each word that I spoke; I took their silence for acquiescence; I made a bow and ran to find Manon. On the way back, I advised her on how she should approach them. – "You are going to see just how much I love you," she replied to me.

We arrive: Madame Parangon and her two friends were still seated where I had left them. Manon quits my hand as soon as she sees her cousin, timidly advances toward her; but seeing her eyes harden, instead of embracing her, she falls to her knees and takes one of her hands. – "Eh, but!" said Madame Parangon, "I have no idea what you want from me: what are you doing, Mademoiselle!..." – "My dear, my generous relative," Manon interrupted her, "my happiness and my tranquility depend on the pardon that I hope to receive from you." – "I forgive you for everything, Mademoiselle! Ah! all is forgiven, a long time ago. Get up; it is unbecoming for a beautiful girl like yourself." – "I have only two options here, my cousin." – "What do you mean?" – "That you must either leave me at your knees, or grant me asylum in your embrace. My cousin, I adore you; in these tears that I shed, witness the pain and the repentance. Ah!

let me bring back to your heart those feelings that you showed me so many times: forget an error that I detest; suffer me to love you, and soon I will be worthy of it. No, whatever my repentance and tenderness, I will never believe myself to be worthy of my husband's love if I cannot recover your esteem and friendship. Bound by indissoluble ties to him, whom I love more than my life, in his arms even, I find that I am lacking in happiness..." – "You are married!" – "Yes, my cousin, and this is my husband." – "Edmond!" – "The very same." – "O, heaven!" – "You know my secret; my fate is in your hands." – "I will not abuse it, Mademoiselle; no, I will not abuse it, despite... Edmond! What am I to think of you? But, what am I to say!... You are married... you were?... How can this be?" – I responded that "before my parents went home again, they had left their signature on various documents; with everything found to be in good legal form, the fear of causing Manon's death had determined me to submit to pressing solicitations; that since my return from my parents' house, on seeing my spouse, her feelings, the dispositions that she had shown me, and her behavior, had all stirred in my heart feelings authorized by duty." – "I cannot get over it," replied Madame Parangon, looking first at Manon and then at my sister. "Fundamentally, he is right, my child," she said to the latter: the motive that determined him is to be praised; and Manon is no longer a criminal..." – I am not quite sure what she meant by that; then, interrupting herself, she said, "Ursule, embrace your sister." At this moment, I noticed in my charming cousin (to whom I gave this name for the first time) so much respect and attachment, so vivid a gratitude, that she said to me, smiling, that she was pleased with me. Oh! what an adorable woman! she is a dove without any bile, a soul made to love and be loved; there is no virtue like hers; if all women resembled her, there would be no more vicious people on earth. Have you noticed that she did not ask for anything in return for the reconciliation? She said to her cousin, "Well, be happy then: an honest and legitimate love is the unique source of our happiness; a woman can find elsewhere only the deceitful appearance of it, under which hides shame, crime, and remorse; never forget it, my cousin. If my friendship can sustain you, I grant it to you; deserve it, by loving your husband; be my companion, as you both desire it; I take on the responsibility of leading Edmond's family back; this lovely girl here will assist me: Isn't that right, my Ursule?" – "How could I hesitate, Madame," she replied, "from the moment that I see in this Lady my Sister and your friend?" – And addressing herself to my wife, she said: "It must really be true, dear sister, that you have a real merit, and virtues, because you have won my brother's heart."

The young Fanchette entered the room just as Ursule was uttering these last words; she was introduced to her cousin, and the conversation changed. As I have told you, this child is charming, and if the thing had not been done, I feel that it would not have been difficult for me to pursue her sister's plan. How I admire her, that adorable sister! after the intentions that I know she has; when the young one arrives, whom she was preparing to introduce to me, to sound out my feelings, – all her dashed plans do not embitter her! She forgives; she does more than that, she wants to serve us!... She makes me feel regret for being happy: ah! how delicious it would be to have sacrificed my happiness for her!

The rest of the day was spent extremely agreeably. I led my wife home again at about the time that M. Parangon was supposed to return: on arriving home, I took less precautions than usual; we dined together; the girl who serves us appeared extremely surprised by our familiarity; it is the first time that she sees me, her mistress herself introducing me [to her]. I was obliged to step out for a moment, and I returned as usual through the small door in back. In several days' time this annoyance will cease, I hope, at least as far as things inside the house go.

I said that I would write to you; everyone sends you their greetings; Mademoiselle Tiennete reminds you of your [need for] prudence; and I, of your friendship.

Two or three days after the date of this Letter, I received a note from M. Loiseau; I could not find it again; but here is the gist of it:

> *All things in good time, my dear M.*
> *R***; life is a moving pageant where-*
> *in one sees the most surprising things*
> *pass before our eyes; and the more*
> *surprising they are, the less we must*
> *hurry our judgment. Often they have*
> *causes that make praiseworthy what,*
> *at first, had not seemed deserving of*

anything but blame. For example, what I have been asked to announce to you: your brother Edmond, my most intimate friend, is married; but you know my feelings, and how far I am from [wishing to] make myself the apologist of a bad action; but your dear brother could not have done otherwise; and as for myself, in my particular situation, I esteem him even more because of it; it is what I protest to you before God. Since Mademoiselle Manon is now his wife, she is virtue itself, etc.

XLVII.

EDMOND TO PIERROT.

He deludes himself, or he wants to delude me, as to his dishonor.

It seems to me, dear older brother, that an insupportable weight has been taken off my shoulders. I love you too much, you know this, not to have suffered immensely for having been obliged to keep quiet with you. In the end, thanks to Madame Parangon, our parents have ratified everything: I am not ignorant of just how much I owe to their indulgence, and that my wedding was non-existent; but assure them, my friend, that they have made the happiness of one of their children. There are two sorts of respectable women in life, dear older brother; those who were always virtuous, and those who having fallen but who find themselves because of their fall even more confirmed on the path of virtue. That so highly vaunted flower, though worth less than nothing,[40] factors so little into what is esteemed in a wife that a young widow is no less ardently pursued than a girl, all things being equal; you will tell me that there is a difference between a widow and a girl who has forgotten herself. I am well aware of it; the former has not violated her duties; she has accorded what was no longer her own; her soul is still virgin and pure; the latter on the other hand has consented to what the laws of society forbade her; she has been either weak, or much worse; but all that says nothing against Mademoiselle Palestine [sic], who was merely seduced at a time in her life when reason was not bolstered by experience. Besides, that lovely woman does not believe herself to be innocent; she groans because of it and is humiliated; she is more complaisant to me because of it; more modest, and sweeter with her peers; the fault, my friend, is more than repaired in my opinion; honestly, I cannot say whether it would have been better if she had not done it.[41]

---

[40]Original footnote: This idea is false; this flower [of chastity before marriage] is a real advantage, and it is to be held in high regard, as it puts a charm into the beloved person's possession. If that is not a real good, then nothing is; but libertines want to lend credit to the dangerous maxim that the flower is worth nothing, so that girls might be less on their guard against their ambushes and corruption. A widow does not possess it; but she has a chastity of the heart, which gives value to that of her body.

[41]Original footnote: all that is just a smoke screen, one cannot be duped by it, after having seen the letters by Manon and the others, which I have in my possession. A pure heart, an irreproachable conduct, infuses an inexpressible sweetness into a

Our marriage, so singularly contracted, has become the talk of the town. Everyone has talked about it; but the conversations that have ensued could not have been further from the truth; the precautions taken by the good Mother Prior of Saint J***, a relative of my wife, forever bury in oblivion what would have been my shame. The very accident that occurred, Manon having injured herself, her advantageous figure, which hid her condition better when she first entered the convent, will forever give the lie to all malicious conjectures. So, may our dear father and our dear mother remain tranquil about it. I urge you to ask them for, and to obtain for me, the grace that I might bring my wife to see them; she so desires it; I believe that seeing her and hearing her will convince them better than anything I could write, about the goodness of her heart; and may they recognize that she was merely young, imprudent, passionate, and the opposite of those indolent and ever lukewarm belles who believe themselves to be models of behavior just because they have no temperament. Yes, my wife is sensitive, voluptuous even (and that's a good quality, in my book), but she is not vicious.

Ursule carries herself well and appears happy through the efforts of her worthy protectress. The city's atmosphere will not be contagious to her; our sister will pick up only its virtues; vice will respect the entrance to a heart that Madame Parangon watches over. She remains at present with Madame Canon, an aunt of my cousin's (Madame Parangon insists that I call her that), whom I have already spoken to you

____

person's life, much more than what my poor brother claims here.

about. That lady is a sort of savage, always holed up at home, declaiming nonstop against men, and against all women who appear to regard our sex with a friendly eye. Ursule is there alright, as much to say that she is safe there: when she goes out, she does not leave Madame Parangon's side. I will admit that, without the society of my respectable cousin, I would be apprehensive lest Madame Canon's eternal sermons did not get on a young person's nerves before too long, to the point where she finds friendly those about whom she hears so many bad things sullenly spoken. For all that, the risk would be small; and if one wished presently to marry our sister off, there are already several candidates who would not be scorned; but one must leave everything to Madame Parangon's wise judgment.

M. Loiseau, whom you liked so much when he was with us, has finally returned. He has taken those steps that he sometimes spoke to you about, with respect to Mademoiselle Tiennete's family: everything went rather well in a sense: M. Dom***, Tiennete's father, knows where his daughter is. When he learned the news, it was remarked how greatly ulcerated his heart had been; he showed no desire to see her; he merely told the young Dom***, his son, that he was to depart with M. Loiseau in order to be near his sister until her marriage. It is true that after having read the letters by Madame Parangon, and those by the attorney with whom M. Loiseau resides, which were filled with the praises of these young people, he lavished every sort of caress on his future son-in-law; he even said this: "I show you all the tenderness that I had for my daughter; and if I now permit her to call me her father, it is because she will be your wife; for she has cruelly wounded my heart, and it is you who heal the wound: you are a more decent young man than I would have been at your age and in your place: I doubt that I would have married a girl who had forgotten herself enough to abandon her parents, those who raised her, cherished her, and maybe have..." – "Respect your daughter's virtue, Sir," said Loiseau; "the error of having removed herself from the authority of a parent such as yourself (an error which under the circumstances is perhaps excusable) is the only error she has to reproach herself for. She was welcomed by Virtue itself, on the day after she arrived in Au***; her young mistress has assumed the role of the mother whom she left behind; also, Mademoiselle Dom*** has never veered for one second from the behavior that characterizes a well-bred girl. She loves me; I would be unjust to doubt it; however, I have never heard her say so from her own lips; she has never given me the satisfaction of seeing her or hearing her speak, except in the presence of a third person." – "Everything that you say gives me pleasure," said the old Dom***; "but she did cause me great sadness; you are my son; she will be my daughter-in-law. Draw up the papers; I will sign them here and now. Her mother and yours will go to Au*** with you; there is no need for me to attend the marriage ceremony." – Nothing that could be said would sway him. What was even sadder still, because it was a new proof of his anger, was that the contract was not advantageous: Mademoiselle Tiennete was practically disinherited. He who appeared the least bothered by this setback was Loiseau. The two mothers, whose hearts Tiennete had regained since their arrival here, are in despair; they effected a delay to the wedding, which will be unable to take place until after *Quasimodo [Sunday]*, in order to write to M. Dom***, but in vain. Loiseau does not think it appropriate to go and live in Au***; he has arranged to have himself received here as a prosecutor; what convinced him of this was a man of reputation, who is offering him his practice at a very good price. I believe that our friend will uphold his reputation well, as much by his intelligence as by his probity.

The adventures of these lovers make me forget my own. Mademoiselle Tiennete's metamorphosis occurred over the last few days. Madame Parangon, who has really wanted to be reconciled with my wife, had invited her over for dinner; there was Mademoiselle Fanchette, my sister, and several Lady friends of the house. Mademoiselle Tiennete appeared, without anyone expecting her except Ursule, who had assisted her in her toilette of a Demoiselle. Nobody recognized her. My master could not believe his eyes, seeing a new girl in the morning, without having heard mention of the exit of Tiennete, who is so dear to his wife. When everyone sat down to table, he made a thousand polite gestures to the young stranger, and paid many compliments to her about her beauty; it was only the sound of her voice that betrayed her, and which made everyone recognize her. M. Parangon's astonishment redoubled then; he thought it was a carnival game, because the entire assembly laughed whole-heartedly. – "I cannot get over it," he continued; "Mademoiselle is adorable, and if I had known this earlier, she would never have appeared without the finery to which she is no stranger." Then we informed him; and Loiseau, who was with us, told the story of his loves. I saw in M. Parangon's eyes, and in his countenance, all his trouble; he left the table early, and none of us were upset, especially not my wife, who had thought of declining her cousin's invitation because of him.

I will tell you about our friend's marriage at the first opportunity, and I will give you a faithful account of all that might seem to merit some attention. Adieu, my brother; I tenderly embrace your dear companion. My wife sends you her best; write to her in a way that will make her love you; at the present moment, she is afraid of you.

XLVIII.

PIERROT TO MANON.

Letter written to maintain the relationship.

Dear sister; I write this letter to you in order to have the honor of inviting you, on behalf of my father and mother, as well as on that of our families, both my wife's and mine, to come and spend Easter with us. We will be delighted to see you, and above all to get to know you more fully, as is appropriate among close family members such as we are. To this end, dear sister, on your favorable response, my brother Bertrand will prepare to go and fetch you on Holy Saturday, in the covered carriage. Rest assured that, on the part of our father and mother, we have nothing but affection and tenderness for you; and that, on the part of me, personally, there is only what I can say to you in person; for Edmond is my much loved brother because of a certain sympathy that has always existed between us; and you, who are his better half, must judge for yourself what you must mean to me... And with that, here is my wife who wants to have the satisfaction of writing a word to you.

FROM MARIE-JEANNE.

> *I am so looking forward to having you visit us, my dear sister: the little that I've seen of you and the good that those in particular who know you say about you, gives me hope that we will become fast friends. There is not a single day almost that passes without my husband's mother talking about you, and wishing to chat with you, to tell you how much she loves you, and that she shall never have perfect contentment in life until she can show you how much of a tender mother she is to you.*

> *I am, my dear Sister, with an unbounded attachment, etc.*

As for myself, dear sister, I will tell you that what my wife said to you about my mother goes as well for my father. We are good people, on whom real merit has its rights, which you will enjoy, and more than anyone. I have the honor of being, etc.

XLIX.

Manon to d'Arras.

A stream of light.

Here I am just returned from a visit to my husband's parents, or rather from the temple of Good Nature. Those people are worth more than all the people I have seen in my life; in their company, one inhales only candor and innocence: it suffices to live with them to become like them. The thing is done, I have decided not to keep the promise that I made to your friend,[42] which was extorted from me; I no longer want it at all; I absolutely do not want it at all. There is no true happiness, I feel, without a clean conscience, a pure heart. I have had a taste of it, of this type of satisfaction, and I resemble those Europeans who, after having been captured by Savages by chance, remain with them by choice, and no longer wish to leave them. Prejudices, caprice, stupidity, bonhomie, call it whatever you like; but that is my last word on the matter. If he threatens, tell him that I am not afraid. I know how to handle my husband; he will believe whatever I want him to believe, you can be sure of it. I find myself very poorly off for the counsels of my cousin Gaudet; as for yourself, Father d'Arras, I invoke your friendship for M. R***, and I make you our arbiter, on account of your known feelings. Do not for one moment hesitate to notify him of my dispositions; he could come and he would find the reception that awaits him to be extraordinary; by notifying him, he will avoid hearing disagreeable things.

---

[42]Original footnote: M. Parangon.

L.

EDMOND TO PIERROT.

Great deftness on the part of my poor brother to keep Ursule, to make his wife respected, and to speak about his secret passion for Madame Parangon.

I have good news to share with you, my Pierre, and I have no doubt that it will cause you as much joy as it does me. M. Loiseau and Mademoiselle Tiennete were united in matrimony yesterday: the nuptials were more brilliant than anyone had expected: the young people, male and female, who were invited by the groom arrived from Av*** the day before yesterday: his friends and ours were brought together to the effect that we composed a large assembly. You are right to imagine that my wife and sister were not the least among them. It is they who create the joy I feel at this moment. Ursule made a conquest worthy of her in every respect, as fortune and merit are found re-united in the same man. He is a young Counselor at the Presidial: don't let this title frighten you: his be-havior is ruled by the most exact decency; he has not yet spoken with my sister; it is to Madame Parangon that he addressed himself; and it is from her also that I learned about it: Ursule herself is not yet informed; she will not be until the thing is certain; one can sure-ly rely on the prudence of my wife's virtuous cousin; because it is she herself who imposed these same con-ditions on the young lover, who agreed to them; on the other hand, Madame Canon, who was made aware, promised that no other man would approach Ursule. You see, dear older brother, that if this affair succeeds, the benefit to our sister and to us will be great; and if it fails, it will be without disappointment or drawbacks for Ursule. All this must prove to you how precious Madame Parangon's friendship is. I did not know how to express my gratitude to her. My wife, just as touched as I was, kissed her hand, saying to her: "My cousin, the more I know you, the less I find myself worthy of your friendship, and the more I desire it; I almost do not dare to love you, this feeling is so overpowering; but I adore you like a divinity." I saw the tears ready to fall from my beautiful cousin's eyes; she hid her emotion from me, all the while caressing my wife; I saw her resume finally that tender friendship for her and that sweet trust that attached them, in their early years, each to each. That was one thing, and here is another.

Madame Parangon left our side in order to be near Ursule, whom Madame Canon had just escorted in; M. Loiseau, who was looking for me, called me; while he was speaking to me, I saw M. Parangon on the heels of my wife, who went into the garden; a jealous and very violent feeling made me follow them. My wife hastened to reach a vault of hazel trees at the most remote corner of the garden; I took another path and got there before she did; to the effect that I had time to hide myself behind the foliage. Manon, on entering it, sat down; she lifted her eyes to Heaven and the tears flowed down her cheeks. At the end of a moment they stopped; her expression grew animated, and her face shined with serenity; she drew a small locket from her pocket, which I recognized as a gift that I had given to her; she kissed it multiple times, looking at a portrait that was not there when I had given it to her; and that portrait... it was mine; Manon looked at it with loving languor, more eloquent than the most ardent discourses. I was beside myself; I was going to come out and give her the caresses that a portrait could not do, when M. Parangon suddenly appeared. On seeing him, Manon let out a cry of surprise, and fright. – "Have no fear, my beautiful cousin," said the unfaithful husband of the most deserving of wives, "for I come only to express my dissatisfaction with you." – "Leave me be, I beg you," replied Manon, "and spare me from having to hear discourses that cannot but be hateful to me." – "Manon, so that is your gratitude!" – "In the name of God, Monsieur, get away from me! If my misfortune should have it that someone approached us here, that my husband should come to know that..." – "You are afraid of my reproaches." – "It is you who should fear mine: you are unworthy of a wife such as yours." – "My beautiful cousin becomes the advocate of my wife!" – "Your cold irony, Monsieur... But why do I bother speaking with you?... I leave you, Monsieur..." – "No, you will hear me out, at least." – "You dare to keep me!" – "Yes, I dare." – "O, heaven!... This vile audacity is quite like you!" – "'Vile audacity' – whatever; but you will listen to me, and your effort to escape will be useless." – "Tremble, miscreant! Be careful not to push me to the brink: take off, or let me go: leave, your presence... it humiliates me, it confounds me, it is a horrible torment to me.. O my God! I deserve this punishment... Eh! I wonder what Your justice reserves for infamous seducers!" – "You need to let this bitterness out." – "I am unable to hold it in... Would that my husband might appear now... O unhappy man! You seduced my inexperience, abused my youth and sensibility..." – "Your inclination for pleasure, my beautiful lady; your temperament, supposing that I abused it...." – "Do you intend to insult me? Go, it is not a crime to have received sensitive organs by nature; but it was a crime worthy of all punishments to have listened to you without loving you; to have profaned love with you by making it yield to the tumultuous emotion of the senses. Yes, I am sensitive; but you..., cruel man, you made pleasure itself hateful to me, and you would make me detest these same advantages that are destined to seal my happiness, if only..." – "Moderate yourself, beautiful cousin; it was not to excite your anger that I followed you here. As I see it, the thirst for pleasure (on your part) lent me charms; your desires, having been satisfied, no longer enable you to see me with the same eyes. If however you wanted..." – "Listen, Monsieur; the mere willingness to listen to your vile propositions would make me criminal; your presence here, I have told you it already, is a torment; when will you stop?" – "My presence is a torment!... It was not always." – "Eh! I am ashamed, Monsieur." – "You made me a promise..." – "Ever since I loved my husband, what have I promised you?" – "Did you not need to..." – "I need to detest you: let me pass, Monsieur." – "I will not." – "I will shout." – "If you can." – "Yes, I will shout, even if it means my ruin... O wretched man, what do you want!" I believe that he was about to undertake covering her mouth; but the sound that I made on leaving my hiding place so frightened him that he ran off. On reaching my wife, who was in tears, I no longer found him there. On seeing me, her grief redoubled; and seeing in my distraught eyes that I was going to leave her, she fell to my knees, which she embraced tightly; "I am innocent," she said to me, "my dear husband. Believe me that I am." – I lifted her, embracing her. – "Do you believe me?" she asked, fearfully lifting her gaze and looking at me, her eyes filled with tears. "I heard everything, my dear soul," I responded; "I was here before you arrived. I heard everything; your cousin is a monster; and if my respect for a woman... to whom we owe so much gratitude did not hold me back still... Let us content ourselves with never letting him see you again... Manon, today is the happiest day of my life: it makes you worthy of all my attachment." I had barely spoken when I saw Madame Parangon and my sister drawing near to us. I made a sign to Manon to go off with Ursule, and I did not hesitate to catch my cousin up on what had just transpired. She appeared little affected by the infidelity of her husband, but the noble and courageous resistance by Manon satisfied her. And that was precisely what I had hoped for. "Let us go and congratulate her," she said to me; "M. Parangon is the dupe of his own practices; but in this corrupt town, he will find only too many opportunities to compensate." We caught up with Ursule and Manon, and finding ourselves to be of a common accord we decided that my wife, no longer having her mother or sister at home, would spend time at Madame Canon's house beside Ursule, whenever I was at my master's. Manon liked this arrangement, like someone whose desires are anticipated; she whispered in my ear, while laughing, that it was the fate of all those who loved me, to feel the most ardent fondness for Ursule.

You see, my friend, that I can finally hope to be happy. This morning I saw Father d'Arras, who was departing for the convent where my wife had stayed. I will follow the counsel that you had given me some time ago to make him a friend of mine, and not that of my wife. Right before this, he found himself in a house that we were visiting, and he wanted to speak with Ursule; Madame Canon, who does not like Monks, brusquely called her. He came over to say some gentle things to my cousin, then quit her in order to approach Manon. You need not be surprised by this behavior; it is the custom here, and the Father is not the less esteemed because of it. It did not take him long to find a gathering of people who wanted to hear him; a number of women were desirous of it. Madame Canon appears also rather strongly suspicious of M. Gaudet; she examines his every move and never lets him speak more than two words to Ursule, nor even to Mademoiselle Fanchette. Until tomorrow, my dear older brother. I love you with all my heart.

LI.

The same day.

M. Parangon to d'Arras.

Explanation of the previous Letter.

Because Edmond has not recounted to you the scene from the day before yesterday, here it is in a few words, dear Father. Manon was persecuting me since the last time we met, that we should have a conversation that anticipated or dissipated all her husband's suspicions. I was against the idea, because I felt that it was going to expose me a little. In the end, I gave in; an occasion appeared favorable at the wedding; we exited twice together pointlessly; I say pointlessly, and quite pointlessly, because the young Panaché did not follow us, and Madame did not wish to listen to anything I had to say, just as you had predicted. Because she is so capricious, I was not so very put out. But on our third attempt, Edmond having followed us outside, the scene was performed, but performed like something out of the *La Métromanie*,[43] the recognition of M. de l'Empirée with his uncle, I believe. The cheeky girl injected a truth into it that frightens me, and with good reason. It would be rather amusing (that is, for a disinterested person) if Manon had made me come there just to force me to hear her true feelings, and to mock me. Which makes me presume that it is from then on that I would be unable to reach her. My prude of a wife has always had her eye on her; she walks in step between her and the little Ursule; and if that were not enough, she has been put under the Gorgon Canon's watch... Ah! if the pretty country girl wanted to compensate me, I would happily leave the brother to his chaste other half! but it is an impossible thing; that little gem has three virtues instead of one; the old and decrepit virtue of Madame Canon, as sour-tempered and as raucous as Cerberus; the bitter-sweet virtue of my wife; and her own pretty little virtue, which, I believe, would be as manageable as any other, without those two solid supports who make a bogeyman out of everything.

------

[43]*La Métromanie*: a comedy in five acts, written in verse, by Alexis Piron (AD 1689-1773).

So you see, after this performance, that Edmond is perfectly tranquil (apart from the furiousness that my conversation with his wife caused him, and which I wisely walked away from), and thus you must be as happy with me as I am the opposite: however, if Manon had wanted it, we would be happier than ever, despite you. But what I see, or what I am afraid to see, is that I am taken for a dupe, and that I have given the little cousin to that Yokel, to my own detriment. I would be quite upset by it, as you can imagine; for then I would have to swallow the pill and continue, in spite of myself, to act kindly towards someone I detest. Adieu.

LII.

The day after.

Edmond to Pierrot.

Innocence sometimes imposes on innocence.

Here is the conversation that I just now had with Madame Parangon, dear older brother; it is a follow-up to my letter of yesterday. This morning someone came to tell me that she was waiting for me. I went to find her alone. With a sweet air, but a little sad, she made a sign to me to take a seat.

"You are married, Monsieur," she said, after a moment of silence, "and you are happy; you love your spouse, she loves you; may so sweet a state of matrimony continue for the rest of your lives!... You know this, and Tiennete mentioned it to you once, I love you, and I was interested in you well before you came here; it was on account of me that your parents were advised to apprentice you in painting, and to entrust you to M. Parangon's tutelage. Upon seeing you again, on my return, I was confirmed in the design that I had formed to be attached to you by the strongest of bonds; you are young, I did not see your settling down until well into the future, and I destined my sister for you. Heaven has arranged things otherwise; but you have become the husband of a relative; I lose merely one or two degrees of proximity thereby, but I enjoy the satisfaction, so ardently desired, of seeing you happy. So Fanchette's presence here, at present, is pointless; I wanted merely to introduce you to each other, in order to fix you in each other's mind, and to give a point of reference to the vagueness of your desires. And as my father, since he became a widower, could hardly expect to be looked after by a girl just exited from childhood, I am going to send her to the Capital in several days; she will wait there, in an honest retreat, that my aunt will conduct her to, until such time as she is properly formed, in order to become my companion, without risk to her morals; for you know how greatly I fear the insinuations of an unbridled man, like... But I would like Ursule to accompany Fanchette; I see a thousand drawbacks to keeping your lovely sister here: in addition to M. Parangon, who tries to converse with her whenever she visits, she has admirers whom I distrust. Do you consent to having Madame Canon conduct them both [to the Capital]?" – I made a sign of approval, so as not to interrupt her; for she was ravishing me. – "However much delight Ursule's company gives me," she continued, "I am sacrificing it for her own bene-fit. I have already shared this plan with the Counsellor whom I spoke to you about yesterday; he replied to me with several objections, the origin of which I see; but if he really loves Ursule, this separation will not cool his interest; and if it is merely a frivolous passion, a passing infatuation, he is not worthy of our attention. My cousin, without me, you would have already exposed your sister to a great danger: to imagine that you would have suggested to her to take your friend Father d'Arras as a guide!... I respect Religion, and I give it all its due, but it would be a hundred times better not to forgo the certain duties it prescribes, such as not exposing her to his morals. Know, young scatterbrain, that a young Priest, even the most disciplined, must never be allowed to manage young women; that we can never be certain about those whom age has cooled, and that it requires more prudence and practice than you possess to make such a decision. I am a woman. I know from experience with what cynical audacity some of those supposed Doctors of the soul cast greedy looks into the furthest recesses of our hearts, not to remove our vice, but often to assess our weakness, to uproot the seeds of decency. Be wary of all Monks, and even all people of the Church; it is rare that you might find a single person in a thousand who has the proper mind for his station. By my advice, your wife abandoned him... But that's enough on this topic. Do you think that your parents will confirm the power over your sister that they were more than willing to grant me? Write to them on this topic..."

You know quite well what I had to respond to

this adorable woman. I thanked her in my name, and in that of our dear father and mother, assuring her that I was going to write to you immediately.

I was getting ready to take my leave when Madame Loiseau, my wife, and Ursule opened the door to the room where they had been listening to everything we said. My cousin continued, speaking to Manon: "Love him well, this dear husband of yours; forbid him to frequent those who might corrupt his behavior: you know the city and the falsity that reigns here; act so that he can profit by your understanding." I left them, because my cousin told me to hurry and write to you.

This step, which she so willingly encourages, quite entirely proves the injustice of suspicions that one has wanted to inspire in me about the nature of her attachment to my sister. Despite what they must have acquired in terms of knowledge of the human heart, my cousin Gaudet and the Father d'Arras are mistaken; for they cannot want to deceive me. In the depictions they affect to paint for me of the disorders of women, I discover a slightly malign satisfaction; these sorts of conversation please them. But what do I care? I enjoy their company, without picking up their vices. I am even obliged to them for curing me of the prejudice that we develop in the country, as to the sanctity of people of the cloth. At present, I respect the profession, but I despise the majority of individuals who comprise it.

Encourage our dear father and mother to accept everything that Madame Parangon desires; Ursule urges you as much as I do; we embrace your dear wife, and all our brothers and sisters. Do whatever you can in our favor, I repeat: it seems to me that a happy destiny awaits Ursule in Paris.

LIII.

PIERROT TO EDMOND.

His infamy with Laurote is discovered.

Edmond! Edmond! Oh what have you done, you wretch! Oh what have you done! To abuse a girl's youth! To take the honor of a relative and discard it! You, who are married, to deceive and promise to marry! Oh! who is it that has turned your mind then, and corrupted your heart! Laurote, our cousin, Laurote!... We have just been visited by her mother, who is out of her mind, tearing her hair out, cursing the day of my marriage and yours; for they just learned that you are married. It breaks my heart! O Edmond! my miserable brother! What difference does it make if you find your way in the city, but you lose your virtue in the process, and your honor, and do not care for your poor soul! or whether I respect you anymore!

Our parents know everything. That tells you more than you need to know.

LIV.

EDMOND TO D'ARRAS.

He sends him the previous letter, and consults his dangerous friend.

Help me, dear Father, my courage fails me... See what was written to me!... My heart is torn, and my tears cannot flow. And that is not the half of it: my parents, beside themselves, hurl maledictions on my head; they make them heard by the man they sent, a stranger,[44] to Madame Parangon; they had the imprudence to have it told to my wife herself, and to plunge the dagger into her heart!... It is true then that virtue itself, and the horror of vice, when they are not enlightened, do as much harm as the crime itself! Instead of dying... but the thing is done: an inflexible rigidity ruins me; a small amount of indulgence would have saved me... They curse me! I shudder: the curse of a father is terrible, and I have just brought it on myself!... Help me with your counsels, my dear Father; I swear to you that I will follow them to the T. Try to pay a visit to the little Laure, out of love for me; win the minds of the mother and daughter; leave your Religious brethren; fly to my aid, friendship urges you to it; employ everything you have; force them, if possible, to exculpate me... But I rely on your zeal and on your friendship for me... O my Father! How dearly I pay for those several hours of pleasure! It is true, it is true then, that punishment always follows the crime, and that crime drags it behind itself, bound by an iron chain, as the good Curate who raised me said!

---

[44]Original footnote: It is in this way in fact that our countryfolk act, and the nobility itself a century or two ago. If they were angered, they enlisted the first person who came along and told him everything that was in their soul. It is imprudent, to be honest, but it indicates a certain respectable frankness, not to mention that the reprimands of this sort are much more efficacious than those of a secret letter.

I see my wife devouring her tears; I suffer from it, in that she dares not complain; her shame, which I know the cause of, devolves upon my own heart and bitterly distresses it. Madame Parangon does not say one word to me. I would like someone to reproach me; I would exhale at least my sorrow and my remorse. Fortunately, Ursule has just departed for the Capital with the young Fanchette; nobody was able to inform her; that is one less burden... But my wife! Madame Parangon!... Oh! this blow will be fatal to my life's happiness; my terrors tell me so... Adieu, do not wait one instant; fly; your friend has no hope but in you.

P.S. M. Gaudet unfortunately is not here; he is expected tomorrow. Where did he go!?

LV.

MANON TO M. GAUDET.

Wrenching remorse.

Vile author of my misfortunes and my crimes, I finally know you: I just discovered one of your detestable Letters:[45] you counseled Edmond to settle the score... wretched man! You who ruined me, you who dug the pit beneath my feet that the hateful Parangon led me to fall into, – tremble: I will unmask you... I am aware, I am too excessively aware of a misfortune... which I deserved... I admit it before God,... this God that your infamous conduct outrages... I will die because of it; but it will not be death that awaits you; it

---

[45]Original footnote: which is mentioned in letter XLI.

will not be the death of wicked men...[46] Miserable creature, you wanted to vilify Edmond's heart, to make it insensitive to shame... not for me, as you told me, but for yourself... I will enlighten you; he will know everything...

I have just thrown myself at the feet of my crucifix, my cousin; I am no longer the same person. The mortal blow has been struck; but I forgive you. I think on my son with a heart full of sorrow: do not approach him, I forbid it; but recommend him, I beseech you, to the generous Edmond, to my virtuous cousin... One more thing: in the name of yourself, have pity on your soul; have pity on Edmond. I pray to God for you. I am desperate for what I have just done; I should have waited for God to shorten my days as it pleased him... however insupportable they have become to me... Edmond, Edmond whom I adored, Edmond is unfaithful to me!... and I have no right to complain about it!... How I have been sorely punished! Ah! the horrible torment that I endure would suffice for my hell now... And there you have it then, the fruits of crime! O my cousin! from now on he is castigated in life... Edmond pays dearly for the pleasures of a moment; I am more punished still; what must await a wretched corrupter?... Adieu. Reflect on it; it is a dying woman who beseeches you. Adieu, adieu forever.

(Without signature.)

---

[46]Original footnote: Terrible prediction, as we will see from what follows.

LVI.

One hour later.

RESPONSE.

Wherein natural goodness extinguishes vice.

If there is still time, live, live, Madame, in the name of Edmond, live: Edmond loves you, he adores you; I will repair my crimes; I will change; live, or suffer to drag my soul with you into the tomb. Ah! my cousin!... you have made me tremble, and it is the last Letter of yours, it is your resignation that frightens me!... Yes, I seduced Edmond; but, free as I am of prejudices, this was merely to make him happy and you too!... I repeat, live, and the man whom you detest, for you, for you alone and for Edmond, will blind himself, and he will merit your esteem.

P.S. I return from Accolet, where I had gone on some advice that I received. One day earlier and I would have forestalled the evil; fate did not allow it.

LVII.

EDMOND TO PIERROT.

Veritable sorrow.

Insane! We love life! There are moments when we give ourselves over to pleasure! And then, what are we? Miserable wretches. Victims who jump up, waiting for the moment to come to be sacrificed. Some fall, crowned with flowers, under a single blow of the fatal ax; others, consumed by a slow and crueler fire, languish rather than live. O the emptiness of joys and felicities of men!... My brother, I have just lost what I loved, her whom my heart grew attached to, too late. From the time she deserved to be loved, through a sincere return to virtue, I was no longer worthy of her, and Heaven has taken her from me... Ah! why did they have to tell her! why did our parents poison our happy days!... Manon held back her sorrow and her tears; she believed herself certain of being unloved, which she could never be; and that cruel idea hit her even harder than the misdeeds... Her blood has gone cold, the fountains of life have dried up: she is dead; she has perished by my hand and by that of my kin! O superfluous regrets!... If only I could follow her into the grave that my misdeeds dug!

LVIII.

EDMOND TO MADAME PARANGON.

This Letter interests and consoles her.

Respectable and generous friend, I struggle to express how much I feel I owe you; your efforts and your goodness have given me life; the air of this place, which saw me blossom, succeeds in fortifying me: in a few days time, I will be in a state to resume my ordinary practices, and to return to being near you; but I will not postpone, however, obeying your orders, and sharing with you the touching discourse that an unfortunate wife addressed to me during the last moments of her life.

We were alone; she had just gotten into bed. I

draw near: her burning hand seizes mine; she lets out a long sigh. I lower my eyes confusedly. "Monsieur," she says to me, "before too long you will be delivered of a hateful object. I do not complain; Heaven is just: if I had anything to complain about, if I dared to accuse heaven, it would be because it allowed a soul such as your own to be sullied by perjury and infidelity. O my husband! Punishment follows the crime at a delayed but certain step; I am the proof of it: may my example be useful to you!"

"Eh! what has happened!" I cried. "Manon, what have you done?"

"My fate still interests you! I will die happy then!"

"You, die! You, whom I adore! Ah! My wife!..."

"Listen to me; there is no more time for us to deceive each other. Dear friend, let me read into your heart: it is no longer your wife who is speaking to you; our bonds are already broken; it is as a friend, who wishes that her death were somehow useful, given that her life was not worthy of making you happy."

I was beside myself; I was agitated; I wanted to get away: Manon held on to me. Finally, I break away; I send someone to find a doctor; I return to her side.

"Why bother my last moments?" she said to me tranquilly. "I wanted to consecrate them to you, and to you alone. I am not afraid of dying; without the sweetness of being loved, life meant nothing to me. I could no longer abide..."

"Oh! you are loved, dear spouse! I adore you; a blamable inebriation, at a time when I knew you so little, distracted me for several instants. My friend, the love that you inspired in me, true love, has only grown since then; esteem accompanies it; ah! deign not to doubt it."

"Could it be true? And I would have punished you by wishing to immolate myself for your happiness?"

"Ah, cruel woman! The things you make me see! You fill me with horror!"

"My love, I was mistaken... Woe to every woman whose behavior is not irreproachable! Suffering, incertitude, and shame must fill her thoughts every living minute of the day; she cannot have confidence in what she does not esteem. I said to myself: 'I have what I deserve; my fault is an indelible stain, and I am desperate. When the wife is the first to lack decency, she must view the aberrations of a husband without complaining.' O, my dear Edmond! Next time, do not unite your soul with anyone who does not have a pure soul. If I had been innocent, my despair would have been less violent, less fatal. But I said to myself: 'How to restore it? My prestige has been destroyed; he cannot esteem me; the contempt that he has for me has relaxed his mores; it is I who sully a soul that had been pure; I know how to punish myself'; and I have punished myself; for I thought that it was necessary that the bonds that united us be broken, so that you might return to virtue..." – I let out a cry of despair. – "Listen to me," she continued; "profit by this moment while we are still alone. Dear spouse, I beseech you by my tenderness, which was extreme for you from the moment that my love began, by this tenderness that brings my heart back to decency; turn your back on evil men and corruptions; avoid also weak and lost women; watch over yourself; there is no joy or true pleasure except in the bosom of virtue. Keep my memory; distrust the friendship of my cousin Gaudet, and that of Father d'Arras, and... will I say it?... distrust the beauty of my cousin; but throw yourself into her embrace, to let her lead you by her wisdom. She is a woman without faults; she is so perfect that calumny, after having exhausted itself against her, found itself constrained to shut its empoisoned mouth. You reconciled us, it is presently the first of your benefits."

My tears inundated my face; I repeated to her that I was going to follow her to the tomb. She spoke again:

"You loved me! Ah! My dear spouse! I miss life then; and yet, I die happy, if only I did not leave behind a child..."

Some people entered the room. The Physician, the Surgeon, did all they could to save her; but soon they realized... O my respectable friend, forgive me for not finishing...

"I knew quite well that it was useless," said the moribund: "I have just written to my cousin. My dear husband, have pity... on my son."

And those were her last words.

If all my sensibility, adorable cousin, was not due to your friendship, the trouble that Father d'Arras just took for me would greatly affect me. From the moment I informed him about the consequences of my fatal adventure with Laure, he flew to that young person, even though she resides more than five leagues from the convent that he directs; he was able to gain the trust of the mother and her daughter, and took such control over their minds that he engaged them not only to cease their (alas! so well founded!) clamors but also to disappear from their village; he led them himself into the Capital, where he arranged everything, such that they might live in abundance; his desire to oblige me has gone beyond all measure even, and I feel that my heart disavows it; he writes to tell me[47] that he has *convinced Laure to sign, unbeknownst to her mother, a Letter to my parents, by which she accuses herself of having unjustly accused me. The motive* of my friend, he says, *is to reconcile me with my family, and to give my wife to her tranquility again...* Alas! Manon is no longer with us; but he does not know that. How miserable I am! As you can see, everything seems to be working against me, and Laure's innocence is for a second time sacrificed for me, without my deriving any other benefit from it other than the augmentation of my remorse. But what have you to say, my dear cousin, about this motive?

---

[47]Original footnote: This letter is lost, but I remember having heard it said that all this conduct on the part of the Father was prescribed to him by M. Gaudet; it was even this latter person who arranged everything in Paris, in order to place Laurote in a life of luxury; for he lived in sin with her.

His Letter was already having the effect that he had intended it to have on my parents: they had received it while I was at my wits' end, succored by you alone; it was shown to them; they passed it around. On my arrival here, I hastened to deny it. My older brother's esteem for me has increased because of it; my parents have grown angry with me again; but Laurette is dishonored in the village; she will never be able to go back there. When I wanted to defend her, nobody listened to me; if I had spoken against her, they would have believed me; that's men for you! You and my older brother are all I have now; your friendship, Madame, together with his, is put to the test by everyone. I do not dare, with so great a good, to continue saying that I am unfortunate. Keep your friendship for me, o most worthy of all women! you are above the weaknesses of your sex, and those of mankind; your conduct continues to prove it to me; make me more worthy of that name, then, which you had so many times applied to me, when I was at the gates of the tomb. Ah! I am unable to bring them to my memory again without being moved to tears, those so sweet accents, those touching expressions of yours that restored me to life! – "My friend, do not moderate your sorrow; it only raises you in my esteem... O my friend! let it show, all your gratitude for the woman who adored you... your heart is still virtuous because you are so sensitive... My cousin, let us be afflicted together; let us weep together for a friend, whom we did not really know until we had lost her; we would be monsters if we did not weep for her for the rest of our lives..." – Yes, my beautiful cousin, you are right; but what would I be if I could forget what I owed you! Ah! what would I be!... fortunately, I feel that it is impossible; you are engraved there, in my memory; my death would precede my forgetting it.

LIX.

EDMOND TO GAUDET.

Written in front of me, sincerely perhaps.

My cousin, reasoning cannot prevail over feelings; I feel, and that is stronger than being convinced of something. Add some virtue, in place of all the vice, and were we not happy? *Feelings lead people astray*, you will say to me, as you have already done; *it can be the product of error, as well as of truth*. I agree. But answer my question and you will be forced to admit that truth is the source of what I feel. I do not want to reason with you, however, or against you; I am too beneath you; only, I wish to entreat you to act towards me as if you were a good Christian, and as if I were a confirmed devout person. I hope for your affection, and I am, etc.

LX.

RESPONSE.

Drunkenness, pleasure, sorrow, and dementia are four states of mind in which a man does things against his better judgment: you are in one of these four states, and I forgive you for your note, Edmond. Write six lines to Gaudet!... Go on, Monsieur, I deserve to be loved by you, even if you were *a thirty-six karat devout person*; because I love you, and because – of all the pleasures that I can enjoy, – the sweetest by far for me is to bring you pleasure. I will persevere in these feelings for the rest of my life. But to punish you, I will not say any more; like you, I only wish to write six lines; there they are. I am, etc.

LXI.

EDMOND TO PIERROT.

Generosity of Manon's mother. News of Laurote.

Time dulls the intensity of pleasure and that of pain: I am finally more tranquil now, my dear older brother. The first days that followed my arrival here, a relapse was feared. Indeed, I cannot convey to you the emptiness that I felt... I loved her more dearly than I even thought!... How many tears I shed, o my friend! how many tears! And what a sorrowful feeling I felt in my heart, on seeing her mother and sister again! All three of us broke down crying; that was the extent of our conversation. The following day, I sent word to them that I no longer believed it was right for me to keep their bequest, and that I was going to give it back to them. They responded to me simply by inviting me to join them in their profession. I ran to the Monastery, and I asked for my wife's mother in order to argue against her resolution. I was told on her behalf that they would not speak with anyone until after the consummation of their sacrifice. I thought that they would give Madame Parangon an audience; I went to find her; she came, but she could not see them any more than I could. I needed to abandon my plan. Yesterday, they took their vows. Two hours after the ceremony, they sent word to me that they would meet me in the parlor. There, the two of them, with a serene, almost joyful air, gave testimony to me of their complete affection. The daughter withdrew after the mother gave her a sign. Then Madame Palestine said to me: "My dear son, I trust you more than any other person; I know your probity, the feelings that you had for my daughter; also, I disdained all the precautions that the laws ask for, and I did not want to make you hear the request that you are about to hear until I had no more to expect from you but your generosity. You are the possessor of our family's fortune; but you know that an innocent creature... Adopt him, I beg you, here, before God and me: I will be satisfied with merely your word; give it to me, that you will have transferred to him the entirety of his mother's possession, when God will dispose you to; no sooner; for I want you to enjoy it until then." She fell silent. I wept. I swore to her to do as she desired, and I bound myself by oaths that she begged me not to make. I added: "And I leave to you, Madame, the revenue." – "Lower your voice," she replied; "if anyone heard you, you would be the cause of our torment here. I refuse your offer. We have given, just like other Religious; no one shows us any mercy; and if it were possible or permitted to *hoard riches* in my new condition, I would have no other desire than to hand my earnings over to you. Adieu, my dear son. Love me forever: we will never stop offering our vows to Heaven for you, and for your ward. Adieu, my son..."

She closed the curtain. But I remained there for a good quarter of an hour, still in my place, sobbing; for all my grief had come back to me with a violence. I will confess to you, my friend, that if the Cloisters of men were such as I imagined them to be formerly, I would not hesitate to shut myself up in one, in order to weep for my sins. But, o my brother, I know what they are like; they are the picture of Hell: the Superiors there tyrannize over those who are subjected to them, over their thoughts even; it is a hateful theocracy where these people put themselves in the role of God, with respect to their Monks (and this is what the word "theocracy" means); the latter, for their part, do everything in their power to get out from under this revolting despotism, which was born in the burning climates of Arabia and the two Indies, and which is not made for Europeans. I owe this knowledge to Father d'Arras, among many others; he lifted the scales that were still covering my eyes with respect to the disorders and slavery of Monks. He is hardly any better than his peers; but at least he is not a hypocrite.

Madame Parangon herself is expected to conduct Ursule to Paris; it was my wish, as you know, that she changed her plans; but she promised not to delay going to visit her. Recently we have received news from this dear sister of ours;[48] she urges Madame Parangon to keep her promise. She says that she finds herself very satisfied in the Capital, and that nothing is lacking to make her happy except her presence. She complains about my silence. Ursule is ignorant about my misfortunes. Madame Parangon wants

---

[48]Original footnote: This letter from Ursule cannot be found.

to moderate her bitterness about them, by apprising her of them herself. You see, my friend, that I will lose my mistress for a period of time. If anything can console me it is that I cede her to my sister.

Neither Father d'Arras nor M. Gaudet have returned yet from Paris; but the latter writes to me[49] that Laure has given birth to a daughter, and that now, very satisfied to have gotten rid of an incommodious burden, she plans to enjoy every bit of her freedom in the Capital. I do not understand these last words; it is an enigma about which I need to ask Father d'Arras, who is about to arrive there, for an explanation. The pains that my cousin takes for this child have deeply moved me. I entreat her to entrust her pains to a wet nurse whom I am sending, and who is from the same village as my ward; they will be raised together; it is an idea that my beautiful cousin approves of.

My friend, the greatest setbacks in life are not always without some mixture of pleasure. It is true that this little girl, and this consoles me a little, costs me quite dearly! however, I feel my heart exult when I think of her, and the most ardent desire of mine is to be able to hold her. O my brother! why is it that what makes us fathers is sometimes a crime! "Father," it is such a sweet name!... Happy older brother, you will carry it without remorse! whereas for me the crime empoisons the favors of nature, at their source even!...

The Counsellor, Ursule's suitor, came this morning. Madame Parangon apprised him of her trip; he asked for the permission to write Ursule a letter

---

[49]Original footnote: Letter not found.

which he would leave unsealed, and wherein he would assume merely the position of a friend of the family. Request granted. But emboldened by this favor, he proceeded to beseech her that a small present he wanted to give to his mistress be not refused him. My cousin was against it. He made the observation that the distance between them would remove any danger. She was adamant. "At the very least," continued the Counsellor, "you might give it to her without mentioning my name?" Madame Parangon wanted to see the present; it appeared too considerable to her, and she refused. This honest man appeared mortified, and deeply. To be honest, I felt bad for him. But it must be that my cousin is right.

I hear, with a great deal of satisfaction, that my dear sister, your spouse, is getting along famously: convey to her a thousand tender things from me. I absolutely want to be one of the first people to caress your child, just after it is born. My friend, I wish it its father's heart, its lovely mother's virtues, and a friend such as I am to you,

– Your Edmond.

LXII.

THE SAME TO THE SAME.

Edmond's regrets after Madame Parangon's departure for Paris; regrets which his corrupters waste no time in softening.

Here I am now, alone, sad, broken. O my brother!

The most absolute, boring solitude is not the one that is found in the middle of our forests! One is not alone there on a beautiful summer day; one has Nature and all its attractions for company. But real, painful solitude is when a friend departs; those wicked men who remain behind and who encompass us, and all those false women who seek to seduce us, but only succeed in making themselves odious, are not company, but a torment.

My cousin has departed; she will go to see Ursule, it is true; but as for me, I will no longer see her! And all the friendship that I have for my sister cannot compensate for the loss that I now feel. We accompanied her for ten leagues, M. Parangon, M. Loiseau, his wife, and I. In our goodbyes, the eyes that were observing me obliged me to constrain myself; but on our return journey, I fell back from the group in order to let the tears fall freely and copiously. Madame Loiseau, who guessed as much, made her husband understand that she desired him to lead the way with M. Parangon.

She lagged behind, waiting for me. I did not find myself discomfited by her presence in any way, but rather I wept with all my heart. That young person has an excellent character; she makes her husband the happiest of men. It is said that her father, touched by the praises that he hears made about his daughter by all those who know her, is quite ready to accord her the first tenderness; but he awaits only, it is said, her perseverance in goodness. Happy are the people, my dear older brother, who having, like her and like me, given their parents trouble, can efface the memory of it by the practice of virtues! How wonderful her example is, and how encouraged I feel to follow it!

Two days later, I was made aware of Father d'Arras' return. I was not insensitive to the news. It has been a long time since I saw a man to whom I cannot not deny being greatly obliged. I betook myself to his Convent. He received me like a father receives his child. "My faith!" he said to me, stepping forward to embrace me, "I did not feel that I had really returned until now, now that I see you. Eh well, my friend! you look sad to me..." Because I did not say anything in response, he continued. "Forgive me my thoughtlessness, my dear friend; I know that you have more than one thing going on; and that the presence of the warmest friend is not capable of repairing the breach that has recently been made to your poor heart. Your sadness does not displease me; do not hold back before me; if I wish to relieve you of it, it is not by cold counsels and impertinent maxims. While waiting, let us dine together; I will have Father Gardien, Father Vicaire, Brother Sainte-Hermine and another person for dinner; what is more, we will have fine cuisine, the eight-leaf wine that Papa Lieutenant of Saint-Brix *recompensed* me, and a big fire, as you can see. We will cheer you up. Come on, Edmond, with my heart in hand, – and all for you. I am a Monk, but in name only: the only title I assume, and which I might find glory by, among my familiars, is that of a gallant, pleasure's friend, and Edmond's; and this last quality, I would not give it up for all the treasures in the two Indies." – Dear Brother! Whose is the heart that could withstand such openness? I responded to him, and in a manner that satisfied him. He did not wish to hear a single word of thanks from me for the services he had rendered. It was M. Gaudet who had done everything; his only contribution was some counsels.

As he finished saying this, I saw my Cousin himself appear from out of the alcove. "Do not thank me either," Gaudet said, embracing me. "I did it for myself; I followed my heart; it is myself whom I served; and it is only to myself that I am indebted."

After I had thanked him, we spoke about the unfortunate Laurette. "Oh! the good and charming creature!" my cousin said to me; "verily, she is exquisite! Don't worry about her; we have taken care of her; she is content, happy." – "Here," said d'Arras, "is her mother's power of attorney, which M. Gaudet will fill out in his name, because I am dead to the world, civilly speaking, according to our baroque laws; but I will not act any differently while I am alive, and he will have no trouble at all; I am responsible for selling their belongings, and making a tidy sum thereby, which I will surely invest. You see the confidence that they place in me?" – "When he has collected everything," interrupted my Cousin, "I hope to add something of my own savings to the sum, and to make a tidy income from it for her. I tell you again, my dear cousin, I love you a great deal, but I swear to you (and d'Arras knows it well) that this has nothing whatsoever to do with you."

I do not know what to think, dear brother. My Cousin is really a good man; or... a big scoundrel! But one must believe in people's goodness, especially that of one's friends.

The invited Fathers made their appearance. The preparations had an extremely agreeable effect on them. At the table, the guests' enjoyment was re-doubled: I found the wine to be delicious, me who loves it mediocrely; and because it was watered down, it stimulated, instead of inebriation, merely that gentle warmth that dilates the heart, leaving the head free to think. I have never seen more agreeable men than the three Monks; it was their politeness, their worldly behavior, an amenity, a polish in their manners that enchanted me. Little by little, however, the natural man showed through. (We suppress here the details from the original letter.) One thing that pleased me is that Gaudet repeatedly assured us that he respected the bonds of marriage. It is always one less vice in the world not to have shaken the respect that people have for the matrimonial union which gives citizens to the fatherland. I do not think that these conversations prejudice me in any way; on the contrary, they give me useful information and help me to understand the world; it is the benefit that I claim to draw from them.[50]

LXIII.

Edmond to Loiseau.

One will see how Gaudet leads him down a primrose

---

[50]Original note: We suppress here a letter from Edmond for the new year. In it he gave an update on Ursule; he exalted the goodness of Madame Parangon, and he congratulated his parents on their being about to become grandparents on account of their virtuous eldest son, who is, he says, *your lieutenant in our regard.*

*path to vice; and in a Letter herewith, a virtuous
woman who makes an imprudent declaration.*

I will no longer have anyone here with me then, my
dear [Loiseau]; all my friends have abandoned me,
and your father-in-law's reconciliation with his
daughter is a setback for me, my dear friend! I did not
know what a great help you were to me until I lost
you. If my cousin and the dear Father d'Arras leave
me, as they assure me they will be forced to do in
several weeks, I will succumb to boredom; I already
feel in my heart a void that frightens me. But I must
leave my sorrowful tone there, in order to congratulate you, my friend, you and your charming companion: God bless the good Old Man, as he wishes amply
to repair the wrong he did to you, and which would
have been a stain on the virtuous Tiennete's character. Enjoy all your happiness in the heart of your na-
tive region. Your new responsibility as the King's Solicitor will give you the occasion to exercise all those
virtues that I recognize in you: be then, my dear
friend, the support of the poor, the friend of the widow and orphan; avenge in your district the humanity
who are suffering from the hard-heartedness of people of fortune: do not be afraid to go too far in that direction; the idea of a Magistrate who favors the poor
at the expense of the rich is a chimera; you will not
find it anywhere, and I do not tell you to try and realize it: alas! the unfortunate part of humanity does not
have such high expectations; it merely asks not to be
oppressed. But you know what we have often seen,
when you were a member of the Palace here, and how
many times the poor lost for the sole reason that they
were poor. My friend, the lions and tigers of the sands

of Libya are less cruel; the Assassin who robs passersby is less dangerous and culpable than those unworthy Magistrates who tip the scale in their favor because of their rapacity or lust.

But what am I saying, my dear man! It is, as people say, like carrying water to the fountain.[51]

I must confess to you (and at first I hadn't the desire to tell you) that one of the two men I have just named (and you will see quite clearly that it is not the Father [d'Arras]), puts everything at my disposal to assist me in the absence of my friends, and his also, resignedly. You know Mademoiselle Baron, that charming, vivacious, joyous girl, who always appears beaming with graces and smiles; but with whom, it is said, pudor does not always keep faithful company? Eh, well, he introduced us yesterday. "That there," he said into my ear, pointing her out to me, "is an excellent topical [medicine] for all your ills; I will put you in the hands of that Demoiselle, as into those of an experienced physician." – "Perchance," he continued out loud, addressing himself to her, as if she had heard what he had just said, "one will be obliged sometimes to employ the iron and fire; they are inveterate wounds, those of the patient whom I recommend to you; but with some patience, and by following nature, I believe you will be able to bring him around." The beautiful person, who was doubtless made aware in advance of our approach, smiled at the apostrophe, and I was very graciously received by her. We went on a promenade; on our return, we danced, and despite my repugnance, I had to take part

---

[51]Like carrying water to the fountain: like preaching to the choir.

in this divertissement. I found it to be quite insipid; and because boredom was getting the better of me, I retired at an early hour. A real pleasure was waiting for me at the house. I found a letter from our respectable Friend. I will make a copy of it for you: she also permits me to share it with M. and Madame Loiseau.

LETTER FROM MADAME PARANGON TO EDMOND

I have been meaning to write to you, dear Cousin; and if I have waited this long, it is because the things I needed to speak with you about required this delay. You know that there are things one hardly dares to say in person, but which one allows oneself sometimes to put into writing; such is the case wherein I find myself, for some time now.

You are free, Edmond: all our old plans, thought possible at first, abandoned later, are today something more than merely pleasant dreams. You are my Cousin; for all my life I would be happy with this title if I hadn't something sweeter to offer you; you must become my brother: count on it and live in consequence. Fanchette is beautiful; I can see that she will be tender; your sister and I are presently working to attach her to you, and we are making marvelous progress. Edmond, it is a great and difficult thing to be master of oneself; a man would have a better chance of governing an Empire than ruling his passions... My brother (for I am sure, for my own part, that you will be my brother), when the time comes, I will let you read my heart. You complain, Edmond! Your ills do not absorb you then?

Your lovely sister appears happy. The atmosphere in the Capital suits her; you would find her ravishing. I see, when we exit together, all eyes fixed on her; but her eyes fix on nobody. What happy tranquility! I will put all my effort into seeing that that continues to be the case for a long time.

I saw the Counsellor yesterday; if I can believe him, his affairs have brought him here; but if I trust myself, it is Ursule alone. He saw her without having been seen. It is pointless to tell you that he is more taken with her than ever; our charms make a much stronger impression on men than our virtues. He wanted to write immediately to your parents, and to conclude against the wishes of an uncle who has long ago chosen another woman for his nephew, to whom he is supposed to leave a considerable fortune. I held him back. Why the hurry? That great fire can become extinguished in no time at all, and leave a woman unhappy. That is not the fate that I plan for my friend; I want all my experience, all my misfortunes, all my troubles to serve her and to ensure her felicity. She will never be the wife of a man who would feel compelled to sacrifice a part of his fortune for her; that has too many negative consequences.

I have received news from our friend Madame Loiseau; she speaks a great deal about you, which I enjoyed hearing because that proves that she loves you. Tell her how greatly supportive I am of the advantageous changes in her destiny, and assure her that I will write to her at another moment of tranquility; to prove it, you can show her my letter; there are no secrets with so dear a friend. But I write to you at the first free moment I have because you are miserable; the second letter I write will be for her. I really like her reasonable spouse; I trust that epithet will not surprise you; one is Reason itself when one always knows how to keep one's cool as he does. A woman risks much less with a man of that character, than with you, Edmond; I would dare say, she shall be happier.

Nevertheless, if I had to choose;... it is not the most sure man that I would prefer. Perhaps one day I will tell you why; but do not let it go to your head, my reasons could very well accrue to neither your, nor my, honor...

Ah, Lord! There's Madame Canon groaning again! I hear her saying: "Man! to whom could she possibly be writing at such great length? If it is to her husband, there is but one word to say to him, – that he is a brute; and if it is to another, that is very bad!" Let's go, let's go, dear aunt!... My God! Will we all be like that when we are old!?"

Adieu, my Cousin.

My dear Reason Itself, this letter gives more pleasure to me than all the divertissements Gaudet wishes to procure for me.

LXIV.

Pierrot to Edmond.

Birth of my son.

Come home, my brother, we wait for you with impatience, come home to embrace your nephew. The mother is doing well and embraces you with all her heart; and she is the only person here happier than I am. Oh! what a thing is nature! Marie-Jeanne, since she has given birth to a son, sees nothing but him any-more. As for me, so greatly loved just one minute before, I no longer exist; I am looked on with indifference, and it seems that everyone, all creatures, must attend only to her son; and if he let's out a cry, she jumps; and if he sleeps, she admires him; and if he wakens, she kisses him; and if he looks at her, she smiles at him, but what a smile!... you have to see it! O dear little child of mine! since your entry into the world you possess an inestimable treasure, the heart of your mother, that so pure heart where vice has never entered! On writing this to you, my Edmond, I feel myself lifted above myself. Come, dear brother, hurry up; on your arrival here, I will speak with you; for I do not like your dinners with Monks, you understand; and you should know how much that weighs on my mind if I should mention it at a time like this. Let Ursule know the good news, before you depart, so that all our family might share in my contentment at the same time. I wait for you in order to embrace you more tenderly than ever.

Your happy brother and eternal friend, etc.

End of Part Two.

Other Books by the Publisher

Fanchette's Pretty Little Foot by Restif de La Bretonne

Je M'Accuse... by Léon Bloy

My Hospitals & My Prisons by Paul Verlaine

Salvation Through the Jews by Léon Bloy

Words of a Demolitions Contractor by Léon Bloy

Cellulely by Paul Verlaine

Ecclesiastical Laurels by Jacques Rochette de la Morlière

Flowers of Bitumen by Émile Goudeau

Songs for Her & Odes in Her Honor by Paul Verlaine

On Huysmans' Tomb by Léon Bloy

Ten Years a Bohemian by Émile Goudeau

The Soul of Napoleon by Léon Bloy

Blood of the Poor by Léon Bloy

Joan of Arc and Germany by Léon Bloy

A Platonic Love by Paul Alexis

The Revealer of the Globe: Christopher Columbus & His Future Beatification (Part One) by Léon Bloy

An Immodest Proposal by Dr. Helmut Schleppend

The Pornographer by Restif de La Bretonne

Style (Theory and History) by Ernest Hello

On the Threshold of the Apocalypse: 1913-1915 by Léon Bloy

She Who Weeps (Our Lady of La Salette) by Léon Bloy

The Sylph by Claude Prosper Jolyot de Crébillon (*fils*)

Voyage in France by a Frenchman by Paul Verlaine

Ourigan, Oregon by William Clark, Richard Robinson, and anonymous

Drowning by Yu Dafu

Cull of April by Francis Vielé-Griffin

The Misfortune of Monsieur Fraque by Paul Alexis

Fêtes Galantes & Songs Without Words by Paul Verlaine

Joys by Francis Vielé-Griffin

The Son of Louis XVI by Léon Bloy

Septentrion by Jean Raspail

The Resurrection of Villiers de l'Isle-Adam by Léon Bloy

Poems Saturnian by Paul Verlaine

The Biography of Léon Bloy: Memories of a Friend by René Martineau

Fredegund, France: A Book of Poetry, by Richard Robinson

The Good Song by Paul Verlaine

Swans by Francis Vielé-Griffin

Constantinople and Byzantium by Léon Bloy

Enamels and Cameos by Théophile Gautier

Four Years of Captivity in Cochons-sur-Marne: 1900-1904 by Léon Bloy

Dark Minerva: Prolegomena: The Moral Construction of Dante's Divine Comedy by Giovanni Pascoli

What is Fascism: Discourses and Polemics by Giovanni Gentile

The Desperate Man by Léon Bloy

Meditations of a Solitary in 1916 by Léon Bloy

The Ride of Yeldis & Other Poems by Francis Vielé-Griffin

Silvie & The Chimeras by Gérard de Nerval

Italian Nationalism by Enrico Corradini

A Silver-Grey Death and *Drowning* by Yu Dafu

Doctrines of Hatred, Part I: Anti-Semitism by Anatole Leroy-Beaulieu

Rhymes of Joy by Théodore Hannon

Windows and Doors by Richard Robinson

www.ingramcontent.com/pod-product-compliance
Lightning Source LLC
Chambersburg PA
CBHW061805190726
48289CB00007B/2077